Indelible

Book 5 of A New Life Series

Samantha Jacobey

Indelible

Book 5 of A New Life Series

Samantha Jacobey

Lavish Publishing, LLC ~ Houston

First Edition
2015 Lavish Publishing, LLC
Book 5 of A New Life Series
All Rights Reserved
Published in the United States by Lavish Publishing, LLC, Houston
Cover Design by: Nicolene Lorette Design
Cover Images: SHUTTERSTOCK
Paperback ISBN
ISBN: **0692277471**
ISBN-13: **978-0692277478**
www.LavishPublishing.com

Table of Contents

Prologue

Running his finger down the list, Enrique leaned against a wall, waiting for Brett and trying to avoid the wind driven snow. Folding the ragged sheet, he tucked it back into his pocket, cupping his hands to blow into them for warmth. *I needs to rewrite it, I guess. It's gettin' pretty worn out.* Needed to, but more than likely wouldn't. It had been written by her hand, and that made the article special, and not for the information it contained.

"Cold enough for ya?" Brett teased as he came around the corner.

"Fuck yeah, le's get some place warm!" he grinned at his friend.

Making it to a coffee shop and finding seats inside, Brett pulled out his own copy of the list, along with the other that he'd been creating. "That's the last 'ne, so we're all set."

The pair had been taking inventory of the lockers for months. Inventory and transfer of the names so that they had clear possession with access to the contents, rent paid on all for five years. "That last stash put us over four mil. I still don' see how those guys put together that kinda cash. An' the weapons. Sons o' bitches coulda started a damned war if they was of a mind to."

Enrique only nodded, fingers wrapped around his mug and gulping the hot liquid eagerly. *I wonder how she's doing.* Pushing the thought out of the way, he struggled to return to the present and focus on the business at hand. "So, what's our next move?" He still followed Brett's lead, even if it was only the two of them left. *Guess that makes me second,* he chuckled inwardly at the irony.

"First off, I say we head some place warm," Brett grinned, tossing his red curls. "Then, we pick us up a couple o' good lookin' girls, an' we settle down for a bit. Play house, if ya get what I mean. Wait an' see, more or less. Hell, we're rich fuckers now, no need o' us doin' anything stupid that'd draw attention to us, jus' in case anyone's lookin'."

Enrique shook his head, "We can't do that. She might need us, ya know?" He didn't say her name, but Brett knew who he meant.

"Man, you gotta get over that," his green eyes flashed with concern, "You said she has your number. If she ever calls, ya know I'd be right there with ya. But she ain't called, an' there ain't no use hangin' around here waitin'." *I loved her too, damn it. But she don' belong to us.* He stared at his friend for a short pause, "It's all we can do, buddy."

The younger man only nodded. *Fuck me. An' fuck her,* angry at his pain. He ran his fingers through his freshly washed waves. "I can't do anything without thinking about her, though. Really sucks when a man can't even takes a shower without rememberin' holding a girl against the wall and pounding the fuck outta her."

"Jesus, man," Brett threw up his hands, "You think you're the only one who ever los' someone? 'sides, she ain't gone forever. If we go have some fun, maybe she'll turn up again." He grinned, "Ya know how she is. She'll get tired o' that life soon enough, an' when she does, we'll be ready."

Brett tapped his list of munitions for emphasis, causing

Enrique to relinquish a small grin, fairly certain he was right. *Yeah, she does enjoy the mayhem, even if she can't admit it. And the sex, can't forget how good she is at that. Or how much she loves life on the road.*

All That Glitters

The five men worked quickly to clean up their mess, the sun threatening to go down before they were ready. It had taken them three whole days to scrape and paint the enormous structure. *Waste of time, if I get my way*, Brian Madson conceded mentally, reaching for the water hose.

He and his bandmates had been hiding in the little town for six weeks, under the protection of Michael Anderson, his newly found brother-in-law. *My God, how fast things can change.*

Previous to their estate being vandalized, and their security team murdered, the band had lived a lavish life, complete with hot women, good food, and all the sex, drugs, and rock-n-roll they could want. *All that glitters, basically*, he laughed to himself. *And now we are here, living like hermits, working our asses off for a girl I don't even like.*

Of course, he didn't really know his younger sibling either, having thought she was dead for twenty years. That, and he was well-practiced at keeping people away, especially women. *If they don't look like someone I'd wanna fuck, that's exactly what they get... shoved to the cold.*

The irony of that thought struck him from the blind side, *holy shit! It's a damn good thing, or I coulda ended up humpin' my sister! A fuckin' Greek tragedy that woulda been!*

Washing the last of the paint out of their pans, his thoughts continued to churn. *Of course, now I have to make amends for treating her like shit, especially if I want to take her home with me.*

They had been waiting for her return, and Brian had become more resolute with each passing day that he would take her with him to New Jersey when everything had been settled. *Set her up in a suite and pamper the shit out of her.* However, he had not told Michael or the others about his plan, mainly as he feared they would try to talk him out of it.

Michael would want to keep his wife and the life they shared. *Hell, he's not fixin' up this gigantic house for no reason.* The other band members wouldn't like the idea either; wouldn't want her to interfere with their lives any more than she already had.

But Brian had used his time in Texas to reflect on his past, and saw that this could be a chance for him to get back something that had been taken from him a long time ago. *Our parents are gone, but I can make her life better. And have the chance to know her.*

That was quickly becoming his priority, and in the last few weeks, he had formulated a plan. *I have a huge house in Florida, my share of the place in New Jersey, and enough money, I can buy her whatever she wants.*

He didn't want to offend Michael, but he felt fairly certain this run down shack wouldn't hold a candle to what he had to offer. *Besides, she's my sister and a musician at heart... she belongs with me.*

Drying his hands, he surveyed the progress of the group, relieved they were going to make it before it became too dark to see. "So, what's for dinner?" he called out jovially.

Michael exhaled loudly, taking in his paint-spattered clothing. Giving his brother-in-law a shrug, "I gotta have a shower before I can even think about eating. You guys can head over to the diner if you want. It don't close for about half an hour. I'll catch up to you or cook myself something at the house."

The rest of the guys tossed their tools aside, eager to be done for the day. Marching down the road, the conversation remained light as they discussed their plans, Cody taking up his role as spokesman for the group, "We're done with the painting, what're we working on next?"

Michael shook his head, "We're taking a few days off. You guys play some music and I'm gonna sit on my ass and do nothing." He hated to admit it, but at thirty-five, that kind of work, from dawn to dusk at hard labor, had been a bit more than he physically enjoyed, even if it gave his mind something to do.

The lead singer grinned at his bodyguard and friend, "Sure thing, old man. Just let us know when you're ready to start the next project."

The group parted ways at the glass door of the diner, the four band members heading inside and taking over the place, eager to get their meal ordered before Trish closed the kitchen. She didn't mind, giving them a warm welcome as they entered, prepared to take care of the group of men.

Michael trudged on towards his current home, the one he and Tori had restored before she went away. Making it into the house, he began to strip, looking forward to the hot steamy cascade. *I'm so glad we bought the tankless water heater.* He had suggested it for her, knowing how much she loved her showers, but tonight, he intended to enjoy the hell out of it.

As soon as the paint had been removed, he leaned the top of his head against the wall, allowing the water to wash over his tired muscles. His mind unwinding, he thought about his wife; *I miss her so much. I wish I had some word on how things were going, or when I could expect her home.* Images of her flittering about in his head, he rested his hand against the wall where he often held her, allowing the idea of her beautiful nakedness to distract him for the moment.

Standing beneath the spray for a good twenty minutes, he finally decided he had had enough. Using the towel to pat himself dry and give his sandy brown curls a good tussle, he slipped into the bedroom to put on his clothes and find something to eat. *Damn. I don't even wanna go back down to the café, and it's probably past closing anyways.* Glancing over at the clock as he pulled on his jeans, he confirmed the time.

Yup, I missed dinner. Oh well, there's a couple of steaks in the fridge, I might as well cook me one of those. Pulling on his shirt, he froze, listening intently. *What the hell? That sounded like my wife, calling my name!* Reaching the bedroom door, he bolted out into the hall, his heart pounding out of control.

Another Mistake

Tori didn't warn anyone about her pending arrival. Accepting a ride with a young man in a cowboy hat, she sat in his pick-up from outside Abilene, all the way to the diner. He had been quite talkative, chattering the entire time about the countryside, his ranch, and whatever popped into his head.

The girl only nodded, uttering small sounds of understanding when it seemed appropriate. *I'm really surprised this guy offered me a ride.* She stared out the window, considering the scar that hadn't been covered in weeks. Usually, no one gave her a second glance when it was exposed; much less let her sit in their car for a four-hour drive. *Must've been desperate for someone to talk to.*

Arriving out front of the familiar structure, "Thanks man; really appreciate it." She managed a tiny smile as she exited the vehicle and closed the door with a thud.

Watching the glow of his tail lights as he pulled away, she waited until he had driven out of sight before she crossed the street and walked briskly down the path. The last greyish pink streaks of the sun were disappearing, and she could feel the tremor she had been fighting the last few nights as she made her journey home. *It'll pass, baby girl. Just gotta hang on and walk towards the light.*

Arriving at the small cottage at the back of the property, she flung open the door and rushed into the kitchen calling his name, looking for the one thing she could cling to. The one thing she knew she could trust. Dropping her pack on the floor and jacket on the back of a chair, she made her way down the narrow passage, "Michael!?!"

Her voice echoed through the small dwelling, giving him a shock and sending his heart into overdrive. He met her in front of the washing machine, in the tiny space between it and the bathroom door, his hair still damp from his shower after the long day of painting.

His eyes were wide with surprise as she walked straight up to him, throwing arms around one another, hugging for dear life. Neither of them spoke at first, and they stood holding on as they rocked side to side. "Oh my God," Michael eventually breathed into her hair, "I can't believe you're here!"

Tori felt a stab of guilt, but pushed the thoughts from her mind as she held him against her. "I'm here." Her voice muffled, she sniffed, unable to stem the flow of tears, *thank God I made it.*

Michael knew she was in pain. He could feel it in the stiffness of her muscles and hear it in the ragged breaths that she drew as she cried. *I'm not gonna ask her what happened,* he promised himself. *She's home, and that's all that matters.*

The couple stood for several minutes, taking each other in, neither of them willing to move. Pushing her back enough to see her face, he laid his right palm against her cheek, massaging the line of her scar affectionately.

"Hi," he breathed airily.

Her face placid, she managed a weak, "Hi," of her own.

His left hand made a slow trek up and down between her shoulder blade and the curve of her rear end, comforting her in silence. Hearing the faint sound of music filtering in from outside, a smile cracked his rugged features and he dropped his hand to lace his fingers with hers, leading her out to the garage while picking his way through the grass in bare feet.

The grin danced on his lips as he walked, tickled at the surprise he had in store for her. Entering through the back door and into the office, the noise of the band increased with every step, causing her innards to vibrate. Guiding her over to the opening in between the two rooms, he stopped so that she could peek in as she listened.

Indelible was there, their new instruments broken in as they played as they had been for weeks. Reaching the end of the piece, the shop fell quiet and the group noticed the couple that stood in the door frame.

Brian immediately burst into overjoyed giggles, popping off the strap to his guitar and dropping it onto the small stand as he pounced over to grab her.

Tori took a step back, holding up her hand to head him off, *oh no, I promised myself to send you packing as soon as I got home. There's no reason to have you hugging on me in the meantime!*

Confused, he stared at her for a several seconds, "Come on, you can't tell me you're not happy to see me!"

She flicked her eyes between her husband and her brother. Turning her back on them, she made her way to the house to climb into the shower, her silence saying all she needed for them to know.

Safe in the tiny room, she felt cold, memories of the last few weeks assaulting her weary mind. Removing her clothes, she felt tormented by the actions she had taken, the hours she had spent with other men, naked in the darkness. *God, I'd give anything for a drink.* Her face drawn by deep lines of regret, for a moment she doubted her ability to

16

remain in the house with the remorse pressing down upon her.

Allowing the water to wash over her body, she recalled that she had taken more lives, men who needed to die. *"You're goin' to hell,"* Dan's voice repeated over and over. *Shut up! You got what you deserved,* she snapped at him angrily. But she knew we all do in the end, and her time would come. *Someday, I'll get mine; there's no getting around it.*

Grasping the small bar, she used the soap on her flesh several times in an attempt to wash away the fresh stains of blood that discolored her fingers. Reminded of her time in the hospital in Chicago, she rested her forehead against the wall and allowed herself to weep.

Eventually, there came a light tap on the door, and her husband called from the other side, "Hey, love; are you hungry?"

Cutting off the warm cascade, she realized she hadn't eaten in a couple of days, and her stomach rumbled to emphasize the point. "Yeah, I could do with a meal."

Her actions slow and deliberate as she dressed, she listened to the voices in the kitchen as they rose and fell cheerily. From the sound of things, everyone was glad she had returned, enthusiastic to hear whatever she had to say. *I don't even deserve this; there's nothing I can share with them.*

Her hair still dripping, she made her way down the hall and joined the group as Michael worked to prepare steaks and vegetables for the two of them. A large bowl of salad sat on the table, and Tori helped herself to a smaller portion and poured the light Italian dressing over it eagerly. Taking a seat, she ate quietly, trying not to scarf the food in haste while listening to their banter.

The five men watched her, her unwillingness to speak

hanging over the group like a dark cloud. They all had an inkling of what she had been about on her little hunting expedition, as Michael had given them enough of her story to pacify the band members while they remained hidden in the tiny town. As a show of respect, they brought their voices down, waiting for either the meal to be ready or her to be ready. In the end, it was the food that finished first.

Michael made a plate and placed it before her, a broad smile on his lips. She glared up at him with doleful eyes, then back at the offering, her heart pounding as if it might explode. Slicing off bites of the meat, she ate the meal greedily, no longer able to control her body's desire to gorge itself.

When she had finished devouring the food, she struggled with the urge to go to the back of the house and hide. Instead, Tori forced herself to sit with the group, not yet ready to share her story, if she ever would be, but unwilling to leave the comfort of their camaraderie.

Listening to the men, their conversation seemed distant, as if it were coming through a wall, muffled by the barrier. With her somber expression to overpower their warmth, the group grew uncomfortable, unable to reach her or understand the pain she refused to share.

"So, sis," Brian attempted to draw her out, "It's good to have you home." He smiled at her, waiting for her to respond. Her cold stare made him uneasy, "I bet it was exciting, going after those guys."

She visibly winced, and the rest of the group audibly gasped at the awkwardness between the siblings.

"Hey, well, look at the time," Cody chimed in. "Maybe we should be on our way, let you guys get caught up in private." Jumping to his feet, he, Chuck and Collin bolted for the door, keen to get to the motel, or at least out of the small house. They had held rooms at the neutral location for weeks, and were relieved to leave the cramped space, made even more depressing by the arrival of the moody female.

Once the room had cleared, Brian made one last attempt, "I'm really glad you're home safely." He held his grin, hoping she would understand.

Tori only glowered at him, clenching her jaw.

He could see the slump of her shoulders, displeasure radiating from her, and a wave of fear overtook him. Standing hurriedly, he stammered, "Well, it's late, I think I'll turn in as well. Goodnight."

Brian had taken up residence in the smaller bedroom, sleeping in Michael's old bed. He went straight to his quarters and closed the door, almost afraid she would try to make him leave if he were not tucked safely inside. After staring at the closed portal for several minutes, he sighed deeply, *well, I guess I get to stay.* Kicking off his shoes and stretching out on the bed, he recalled the evening's events.

She doesn't want me here, he debated mentally as he blinked at the ceiling. *How am I gonna convince her to go home with me if she won't even talk?* Of course, it was her first night back and there would be lots of days to persuade her, as he had no intention of leaving until he had done so.

Meanwhile, Michael led the way into their bedroom, Tori closing the door behind them. Eager to hold his wife, he wanted to comfort her, and welcome her home as only he could. And he needed to return her ring.

He had kept it in his pocket the whole time, waiting for the right moment to make the offer. Flashing his straight white teeth, he opened the pouch, "I have something that belongs to you, missy."

Tori braced herself, feeling the trepidation at what loomed ahead of her. Watching the small circle of silvery white gold slide out onto his open palm, tears spilled over and ran down her face, and she shook her head ever so slightly. *Oh my God, I can't accept it. I don't deserve this man; I'm so dirty and unworthy after what I've done.* She looked up from the treasure, eyes filled with pain.

Seeing her expression, his face relaxed, allowing the smile to fade. "I know this is hard for you. And, I know you aren't ready to talk about it. But this is yours," he held the band up between a thumb and index finger. "I would really like to see it on your hand."

Gazing into Michael's deep brown orbs, she knew what her refusal would mean to him, and relented, silently raising her left arm towards him. Her fingers trembled as he reached to catch her palm and hold her steady while he slid the symbol of his dedication into place.

Smiling at her, he deduced that she felt troubled by the things that had happened and she had taken part in. *We need to talk*, he rationalized, but he already knew she would resist. *She never has been big on sharing what's inside.* "Thank you," he stated firmly, his grin smaller, but genuine. Still holding her hand, he used the appendage to pull her towards him.

Her body pressed against his, Michael could feel the tightness in his chest, fairly certain she had been with other men while she was away. *Either by force or by choice, not all of her came home.* Swallowing back his anger, he reminded himself, *she's still my wife, I still love her, and she's going to share my bed.* At least, he hoped that she would.

"You wanna tell me about it?" he made the offer while rubbing her spine firmly.

"No," she clipped, her voice low and emotionless.

Damn. I knew she wouldn't let me in. Not yet, at least. Adamant at not allowing himself to worry over things they could not change, he tightened his hold even further. Michael still loved and wanted her; the only thing that needed to be said. *If she won't talk, then I'll find another way.*

His cheek pressed against her hair, he whispered next to her ear, "It's ok. I'm here, and I can wait until you're ready."

Sliding her arms around his neck, she exhaled deeply, hugging him against her as her only reply. Hearing her sob, he continued to squeeze, grateful she would at least be able to cry, and that would mean release.

When her tears were spent, Tori pulled away to remove her clothing, and then re-covered herself with her sleeping shorts and a tee. Michael had turned away as she moved, not wanting to look at her nakedness, fearing he would be overcome with desire.

The girl noticed his averted gaze, acknowledging the goodness of her mate, again feeling unworthy of such a man.

Her choices were not a provocative ensemble, and he knew what it meant, even without her saying so. Following her lead, he covered his white briefs with a pair of shorts, and they would lay together as friends that night, allowing each of them to become adjusted to the new scars that she carried on her soul.

Switching off the light, they stretched out on their bed, and Tori allowed her husband to slide his hands across her body. He did not touch her in a sexual way, but the concern he held for her easy to read in the pressure he exerted on her taught muscles. Rolling onto her belly, she felt torn by shame at the pleasure his hands held against her.

Massaging her arms and legs, he breathed deeply in a steady pattern, and she began to inhale and exhale in a slow rhythm. Using the large flat area of his hands, he pushed heavily, then pinched larger sections between fingers and palms, kneading her as if she were a lump of dough for a loaf of bread. His movements were intoxicating, and Tori relaxed into his caresses.

Working the muscles that covered her ribs and back, Michael could feel her beginning to calm herself. A boyish grin crossed his lips as he swung his leg over her and squatted on the backs of her thighs so he could press down using his weight. Pushing heavily on her buttocks with the heels of his hands, he caused her legs to tense and spasm slightly, then unwind, completely refreshed.

Brushing a few loose hairs out of the way, the fire that she kindled within him raged out of control. *Shit*. He wanted her in the worst way, the evidence suddenly becoming more than he could hide.

Trying to be respectful of her needs, he slid to the side and stretched out next to her, his right hand continuing to move up and down the length of her back. She lay facing him, her eyes closed, and he wondered if she had fallen asleep during his comforting strokes. He released a deep sigh, *I wish I could make her see how much I love her*, not realizing he already had.

Feeling his breath on her face, Tori lifted her lids and stared at him. Pushing herself up on her elbow, she gazed at his perfect lips for a moment, and he watched her deep blue eyes, patiently waiting for what she needed to say.

"I have done… some terrible things," she finally admitted. She had never intended to tell him about her transgressions, but lying with him, she knew she had no choice, as he deserved to hear the truth.

Drawing a ragged breath, she continued, "I'm not even sure all of them were necessary. I just… got caught up somehow, in the place that I was and the role that I was playing. I let them do things to me that a wife should never have done, and I'm truly sorry." She blinked at him calmly, gentle blue pools filled with agony.

His right hand stroking the line of her jaw, he whispered, "It's ok. I know how difficult it was for you."

He really didn't, and it bothered him that she had used the words *role that I was playing*, as if she weren't really a person and everything she did, an act. He had felt that way about her when they first met; only seen her as conniving and untrustworthy. It concerned him to be reminded of that side of her he did not want to see as her true self.

Feeling reassured by his understanding, Tori ran her fingers across the hair that blanketed his chest. Pushing the images of the others from her mind, she leaned over to nuzzle his face, and then kissed him as she gripped him more firmly. Michael parted his lips, allowing the kiss to deepen, sliding his hands over to indicate his desire to remove her shirt.

Moving to comply, Tori pushed herself up further, onto her knees, and he sat up next to her, lifting the garment over her head. Her breasts were beautiful, her pink rose displayed brightly in the pale light that shone in through the wide window next to their bed. Using a finger, he lightly traced the shadow of his name that she wore over her heart, and felt guilty that he had judged her in his thoughts so harshly.

Of course, this isn't just a role, and it's unfair for me to expect her to be like other women. She's not, nor will she ever be, like other women. Her life had molded her, and created this uniqueness that caused him to cherish her so deeply. She had been made for him, and although others had tasted her flesh, none could touch her heart as he had, and he accepted this about her in full.

Running his hands across her rounded forms, he brought her nipples into hard pink points, and her breathing changed once more as he awoke her desire.

Tori could feel her soft folds growing moist, and she grabbed her shorts and panties, sliding them off with haste. She had avoided the alcohol, but there would be no way in hell she could resist the temptation of his flesh.

Rising above her, Michael removed his own clothing and pushed her over onto her back, parting her legs. He couldn't wait any longer to find his way inside her. Holding himself above her with locked arms, he took her with deep even strokes, dipping to kiss her as his hips pushed against her thighs.

Pulling her legs back, Tori longed for him to punish her, to pound her and take her in ways he never had. Clawing at his back, she tried to encourage him to drive against her with greater force. Pulling down on his shoulders and running her hands along his back to squeeze his naked rear, she wanted him to push harder, faster, to make her scream, and tremble beneath him. Gazing past his brown orbs, she glared at the darkness above them, unworthy of his tenderness.

Closing her eyes, she gave herself to him in the night, the best that she had to offer. *Harder, harder, please! Hurt me, baby... hurt me good*, she inwardly begged. But Michael wasn't the kind to hurt who he made love to, and in the end, their actions left her feeling empty. Reminded of the last night she spent with Enrique, she felt as if she had made another mistake, and lay in the wrong bed again.

No Rest for the Weary

Lying in the early morning light, Tori faced the window, her husband breathing deeply to her back. She had his ring on her finger, pulled out to the end so that she could turn it and play with it while she stared at the smooth, shiny surface; her mind combing over the day he had given it to her. She had placed her faith in him, because he had been so certain that they belonged together, his message still crystal clear inside the band: *For Tori, love of my life.*

Toying with the ring, she realized she had no real feelings on the matter. She lay with him because fate had seemed to be pushing her that way. The date, April first, Henry's brother, and the loving way he regarded her. It had become a muddled conundrum, a puzzle with no solution. Taking a deep breath, she closed her eyes and willed her mind to clear.

That isn't true; I did have feelings. She had loved him dearly before the plane ride to New York. If that had not happened, they would be lying somewhere together at that moment, as deeply in love as ever. Of course, the danger would still be around them, and that would be the one good thing that had come from the events of the last seven weeks or so.

The Scorpions were gone and the couple could move

forward with their lives in peace. *I will love him again, in time; I have to be patient until the feelings return.* Until then, she would do everything in her power to convince him her love remained strong. *I must do this… I cannot allow him to be hurt by my callousness.*

She had made men feel she cared for them before, she had no doubt she could do it again. Besides, what they had being most precious to her, she felt it imperative that he never doubt her devotion to him. Sliding his ring back into its proper position, she rolled over to face him.

Michael lay with his back turned to her, and as she spooned up behind him, she felt a tickle of excitement in her stomach. Sliding her arm over his side, she pushed her fingers up through the thick mat that covered his chest. Failing to get the desired response, she slid her hand down and grasped his manhood firmly.

Finding it flaccid startled her slightly, but she massaged it patiently, bringing it to life. Pulling on his side to roll him over, she straddled his legs, her wet hollow resting on his knee as she took him inside her mouth.

Michael awoke to the eager caresses of his wife's hand and tongue, a bit surprised by her desire as she had seemed rather unhappy about their lovemaking the previous night. He had done his best to go through the motions for her sake, not wanting to stop once they had started and cause her any more grief than she had already endured.

Touching the top of her head, he signaled to her that he was awake and ready to become an active participant in her activities. Looking up at him, not ready to relinquish her prize, she breathed a small laugh, some of her old feelings of joy briefly lifting her spirits.

Rubbing her delicate female parts against his knee, she trapped her small pea between her pubic bone and his kneecap, causing her need to grow more urgent as she worked the tender spot.

Raising his head and chest, he aptly slid his fingers around her rear end. He allowed them to slither into her, the wetness beyond belief, evidence she truly felt excited to be with him at that moment.

Aware she would push him over the edge, he abruptly grasped her chin, raising her mouth and grabbing himself firmly to try and hold off the inevitable eruption. As soon as the urgency passed, he gripped her by the forearms and pulled her heavily on top of him.

Grasping her hips with both hands, he drove himself into her from the lying position. He loved the noises that she made, knowing she had fallen into the moment just as deeply, and he focused hard, not finishing until she had clawed at him and panted in her usual way. "God, it feels so good when you get yours, the sounds and feel of you are such a rush," he whispered against her hair.

Pushing through her ecstasy, Michael finished himself as well, squeezing the skin that covered her ribs with lust, and she relished in the pain of his fulfillment. *Oh my God, that's it, love, mark me… make me yours!*

Allowed to lay over him, she kissed the side of his neck, whispering, "I love you so much. Thank you." Her words surprised him, as she did not often speak to him so affectionately, and he hugged her tightly, grateful to have her and knowing it must be true.

Catching her jaw to look her in the eye, "I love you too, Mrs. Anderson." He grinned at his own admission, cheerful at their returning tenderness.

Lying together for some time, the couple allowed their hands to explore each other while the warm afterglow subsided. Eventually standing, Tori helped her mate to his feet and cooed into the soft front of his neck as he hugged her. *See? I feel more fondly of him already*, and this reinforced her belief that she would, in fact, love him again, if she could be patient enough to allow it to happen.

Moving to the door, the couple peeked out to see if Brian would be waiting, but seeing the entrance to his room standing ajar, Michael surmised that their noisy encounter had driven him from the house. Slipping into the bathroom, they showered together as they had done on the day they were married, and he felt obliged to claim her against the wall, as he had done that day as well.

Tori giggled joyously at his silliness, eager to have him inside her. She relaxed against the tile and stared into his eyes with a small smile curling her lips as he satisfied himself beneath the warm spray. She wanted to love him, needed to love him, in a way she could not put into words.

Drying themselves, they dressed and went out to find the band gathered in their living room. The group spoke quietly, there seeming to be a great deal of tension between the men. Seeing the couple exit the hallway, their voices died away, and they stared at the tall, dark haired woman dubiously.

They had never seen the scar that marred her face until yesterday, and although Michael had shared some of her story with them, he had not given them much to prepare for the sight of it. She did not smile, nodding to them, "So, when will you be leaving?" She addressed the group as a whole, her tone completely void of emotion.

Michael had stopped in the kitchen to gather breakfast for them, but paused to glare at her, having heard the coldness of her words. He felt surprised she would be so eager to get rid of the only family member she had found, and then recalled that she didn't know about the DNA test and that their connection had been confirmed.

Moving over to join the group, he mustered an excited tone, "Look, love; guess what we've got!" He produced the envelope that Warren La Buff had presented to them on his visit about four weeks prior.

Tori only stared without touching it, already knowing what they had required proof to believe. Looking back at her brother, she drew a deep breath before she spoke. "Your name isn't Brian Madson is it?" She uttered the words as if they were a statement as she already knew the answer.

He stared at her, not sure what she thought or why she asked. Her voice sounded angry and confused him further as to her motives. Finally, he shook his head, "No, my name is Daniel Peters. I changed it when we cut the first album."

Tori nodded, staring at him as she considered this. She had begun to have memories, small and intermittent. *I shared many of them with Brett; more than I should have.* She got the impression her brother had not liked her when they were kids any more than he had liked her before he knew her identity. Shaking her head, she raised an eyebrow at him, "It's time for you to go home."

Walking over to the kitchen, she began to help with breakfast for her husband and herself, "Here, baby; let me make the eggs."

Michael gazed at his wife as she talked to him sweetly and smiled at him whenever she looked his way. *And she just called me baby. Well, fuck me, this is an act after all.* Looking down his nose at her, he recalled her reassurance before their shower. *I wonder who she's trying to convince, me or herself.*

The band busily agreed with her, Cody taking up the cause, "Come on man, it's time we headed for home. The group that vandalized our place has been dealt with, and we all have lives to get back to."

Brian only stared at his lead singer with a slack jaw, trying to decide how to break the news to them without giving away too much of his plan. "I'm not leaving until she tells us what happened. Forgive me, but I don't see *dealt with* as being enough proof for me that we're really safe."

Tori ignored his request, unwilling to share the details with anyone, even Michael. Continuing with the business of cooking the eggs, she decided to add bacon to the menu, and pulled the package out of the fridge, dropping it on the counter with a thud.

Collin joined in, trying to help motivate their guitarist, "Come on, man; you can't tell me you wanna stay here. In this hick town? Sister or not, we got better things to do. And if it ain't obvious enough for ya, she don't want you here." He pointed a thumb over at the girl to emphasize his point.

Brian chewed the inside of his cheek, feeling the anger simmering within him. *Who gives a fuck what she wants? I have a say in this too, God dammit!* "Yeah, I can see she's not thrilled with the idea," he exhaled loudly, continuing to be diplomatic, "But like I said, I'm not leaving until I'm satisfied, and there isn't a person in this house capable of convincing me otherwise."

"Either way, you three are free to go," he stood up abruptly, intending to put an end to the debate, "Good luck to you, and I'll see you if and when I make it home." With swift jerky movements, he headed down the hall.

Going to his bedroom, he closed the door loudly and sat on the bed, staring at it, waiting for Michael to come and tell him he had to leave. Soon, he could hear voices raised, and he realized that his sister and her husband were shouting at one another. Opening the door, he leaned out into the hall while keeping his feet on the carpet to listen.

"You can't throw him out. Half this house is mine, and I say he can stay!" Michael hadn't raised his voice at her in almost a year, not since their journey from California. Feeling a stab of guilt at her pained expression, he tried another track, "Just let him stay a few weeks, now that you're here. He'll be satisfied and then get bored. He'll go home and we can be alone."

Brian couldn't hear her reply, so he assumed that she had either lowered her voice, aware that he could hear, or she had given up on the argument. *Wow, I can't believe he's standing up for me,* he muttered to himself. *He won't be very happy he did that when he finds out I'm not leaving without her.*

Out in the front room, Tori wasn't so sure about Michael's assessment. Her emotions churning, she wondered why he would want to stay, and why her husband would take his side. She felt hurt that he didn't have her back in this.

In the end, the two men won, and they agreed that he would stay for a month, and then return home. *No rest for the weary*, she thought as she ate her eggs and bacon in brooding silence.

Finding Yesterday

Tori didn't like Brian being in her house. However, she didn't like arguing with her husband more, so in the end she had allowed the man to stay. Being five years older than her, he remembered her life before the Dragons had taken her, a fact that troubled her deeply. *I don't care what he knows; I don't wanna talk to him, to know him, or to be close to him.*

The band put their instruments into a storage unit and left town, putting all of Tori's tools and items back into her shop the best they could. As soon as they were gone, she surveyed the damage in disgust and set to work putting things in order.

Once the garage had been put back to normal, she continued to spend her time there working on her projects, but mostly hiding from Brian. He left her alone while he and Michael quietly put a few more touches on Marge's stately structure. She didn't bother to inquire what they were up to, only glad that he let her be.

However, after three days, he followed her into her haven and took up a seat to watch. At first she ignored him, but soon his curiosity got the better of him and he moved in closer to have a better view.

She squatted next to a half-stripped machine, and he

peered over her shoulder so he could observe her while she worked. She knew his questions were coming. *Sorry bastard. Go the fuck home, already.*

He started by inquiring about the bike itself. "So, what kind of bike is this?"

"'86 Honda." She bit the words sharply.

"Oh yeah?" his voice lifted in pitch slightly, "Well, how fast does it go?"

"Fast." The lines dug into her face as she frowned.

He continued for several minutes. Tori ignored questions that required more than two-word answers, fuming as her fingers moved.

Eventually, he stopped talking and simply stared at her. "Why're you so angry at me?" he finally asked in a calm voice.

Holding her wrench suspended in frozen motion, Tori dropped her shoulders in disgust. She honestly didn't know the answer to that question. Turning her head to look at him, arms still hanging in front of her, she considered what to say carefully.

"Don't feel special," she finally muttered, "I'm angry at everyone."

Her reply made him smile and he bobbed his head in agreement. "I get that. You had a hard life. And you always were stubborn."

His assessment shocked her, reminding her how Eddie had said the same thing. Dropping her eyes, she lowered her tool and placed it on the grease stained cloth, next to the rest of the utensils she needed at the moment.

"I don't remember much about it," her tone quiet, she kept her focus on the bike. "I remember our parents, I think, but only a small thing. And I remember you. I was following you, and you were shouting at me to go away, saying that I was annoying." Her voice cracked a little, as if the memory caused her pain.

"Yeah," he breathed his reply, "I was a real jerk. You used to love to follow me around and asked so many questions." She turned her face to peer at him again, and he smiled. "I really am glad to get a second chance. I know you want me to leave, but," he shrugged, "I can't do that yet."

Tori only nodded, standing and moving over to the long bench of tools to straighten it, not that it needed straightening. She had promised herself she would stay away from him; that she didn't need to know about those days that were gone forever. *He's family in name only, and Michael's all that I need,* she reminded herself sternly.

Moving to position himself beside her once more, Brian pushed the issue. "What would it hurt for us to be friends?" he asked with a hushed air.

Tori busied her hands with the tools.

"You know," he watched her movements, "I'm pretty sure that's about as good as they're gonna look."

She stopped and laid her palms flat on the table, cutting her eyes over at him. "What good would it be?" she put the question to him in a frosty manner. "I can never get that time back, Danny. I can never be young again. Won't ever have a family of my own. What good does it do to act like this is a second chance?"

He backed away from her, a large grin spreading across his face.

Tori's expression changed to bewilderment. "What the hell are you smiling at?"

He squinted slightly, nodding his head, "You just called me Danny. You *do* remember me."

Flicking her gaze to the wall in front of her, she started to deny it, but something in his voice caused her to remain silent, so he continued. "Don't you think our parents would want us to be close? I mean, as many times as they told me to stop hiding from you or stop picking on you; I sure think they would. If not close, at least friends." Shuffling his hands nervously, he took another step back. "I'll let you think about that for a bit, *Nikki*." He still smiled as he went out through the wide door and headed to the café.

Touching the tools again absently, Tori allowed herself to go over the conversation in her mind. *I called him Danny.* For some reason, that was his name now, and she couldn't explain it. She only had the few memories of their parents and had not bothered to tell him they were from the day they died, specifically of the crash and the burning car.

She had dreamt the scene again several times since discovering her identity, and her parents were screaming and talking before the fire; Tori felt pretty certain they were shot before the blaze had been set. It saddened her to think about it, and she could not bring herself to share that pain with him.

Inhaling deeply, she realized that was the real reason she wanted to keep him away. *I don't want to share my misery with him. For one, I'm still not certain that he really cares.*

Having met him as a stranger, she didn't see him as that kind of person, and her new-found memories had done little to alter that opinion. *Two, having heard about my life from Michael, or whoever, isn't the same as me telling him about all the things that happened to me.*

The time had come for Tori to face the facts and admit to herself that she was ashamed of her life. Mortified by the things that she could not stop and of the things she did that brought pain to other people. *I'm a murdering whore, after all, no matter how you slice it.*

Michael understood those things because of his own experiences and because he had seen her life firsthand. *My brother will never understand. No one really will. Hell, I lived it and I'm not even sure I understand it,* she confessed to herself.

Allowing a weary sigh to escape her, Tori knew what she had to do. Finding out about the past would be an essential part of healing, and she did want to heal. Learning to face her fears would be a part of that, and it felt like a razor sharp blade that cut her into two halves; the half that *feared* being judged, and the half that *wanted* to be judged.

Turning to the roll up door, she grabbed the rope and pulled it closed, not bothering to lock it. Walking towards the diner, she practiced what she wanted to say. Her heart pounding, she recalled the day she had to ask Eddie about washing her clothes and had gotten her first lesson on motorcycles, which was a disaster.

Entering the tiny eatery, she wiped her sweaty palms on her jeans. Brian sat on a stool at the counter, laughing and talking with Trish and her boys. It had been a long time since Tori had talked to the pair of young men, and she wondered if they were avoiding her since her return.

Seeing her come in, Christopher's smile tightened, and he made an excuse to leave, pulling his brother with him. Curious what they had been told that made them afraid to talk to her, she could only speculate at the moment. *That'll have to be dealt with some other time*, she acknowledged with another cleansing sigh.

Steadying herself by clenching her fists, she took the vacated seat next to Brian and ordered a glass of water. Playing it cool, he waited for her to make the first move. Trish gave her a tiny grin, unusually quiet as she placed the frosty container on the counter and opting to clean tables directly so the two could have some privacy.

"Well," she chose a seemingly harmless theme, "I see you and the boys are getting along nicely. They used to come to the house every day, back before I had to go away. Now they don't have anything to say to me."

Giving her a sideways look, "Is that really what you came down here to talk about?"

Tori allowed him a small smile, "Of course not, but it's a much safer topic."

He returned the grin, knowing exactly what she meant. He had learned how to stick to the safe subjects over the years, hardly ever telling people what really went on inside him.

Avoiding looking at him, she tried again, "So, how does this friend thing work exactly? You know, I haven't had much experience in that department, and people who're close to me tend to end up dead." *F-F-Fuck.* That didn't come out the way she planned. *Too late now, damn it.* She swung her gaze towards him, waiting nervously for his reply.

Brian studied her delicate features, not really sure how to respond to that. After a tangible silence, he decided to go with brutal honesty. "You know, I just don't get you sometimes. I guess that's what the *friend thing* is all about. I just want to get to know you, and maybe understand you a little better. And not from second-hand stories, either. I want to hear about you *from* you. Whatever you're willing to share."

Tori only stared, nodding slightly. Remembering that he spoke French, she changed languages, causing a confused expression to flutter across his face. "I'm crazy," she told him matter-of-factly. "At least, I'm pretty sure that I am."

Translating what she had said, he burst out laughing, raising his glass in a toast to her, "Well that makes two of us. I'm glad that gives us some common ground." His usage not as smooth, it had obviously been a long time since he really practiced it.

She emitted a small laugh with him, the sound strange to her. She had learned to smile again, but actual laughter was still pretty rare. "I sometimes feel like I'm borrowing other people's emotions," she confessed, sticking with the French. "I spent a long time pretending like I didn't have any, as if I was invincible or something. No happy, no sad. Just, nothing."

Brian wasn't sure where she was going with the comment, but it was a start. *That's the thing about searching for yesterday, you never know what you're gonna find.* "It's a self-preservation thing I think, like protecting yourself. I get it." He nodded in an exaggerated fashion, and she believed he did.

Gulping down her water, she suggested they return to the shop and she would show him some things about the bike she had been working on, "Since you seem so interested."

Holding up his hand, he made a stipulation, "Only if you let me show you something in return. How about music?"

"Is that a jab at my ability to play?" her nose scrunched, shocked he would say such a thing to her, especially when they were learning to get along.

Shaking his head, he grinned deviously, "No, silly; you don't read or write music. I would love to teach you, so you can put all those songs you wrote down on paper properly."

Tori's face went stone cold. *He's been snooping in my stuff.*

As if he had read her thoughts, he shook his head, "Wow, I am totally fucked, either way I go here. I guess I'll take the blame on that one."

"What do you mean by that?" she demanded curtly.

Looking away, he tried to be nonchalant, "Michael was really proud of your work. He showed me your spiral full of songs. The lyrics were really good, but reading the music was a lot harder. I could help you with that if you let me."

He paused for a moment, giving her time to grasp his compliment, then continued, "I never told you that song you wrote was fantastic. Didn't have a chance, I guess. But yeah, it was pretty incredible. If you had been able to win, you would have."

Tori felt herself smile, not sure if she believed him, but the fact that he actually said it meant a lot. Leaning on the counter, she considered his offer. She knew she would accept it, *what have I got to lose?* She could see her life expanding before her, years and years of it. She had never really thought too far ahead, never dared to dream about the future. Staring into the crystal blue eyes of her closest kin, she had to admit, *maybe, it's time that I started.*

Real Family

The sun moving over into early evening, Michael returned from Marge's house to find the pair working on the bike. He had entered through the office and could hear them in the large shop area, speaking to each other in both French and English for some weird reason. Pausing to listen closer, he could make out that she was teaching him about the tools and the motorcycle at the same time.

The two of them speaking civilly to one another in any language sounded like music to his ears. He had been deeply concerned that they would never see eye to eye, or that she would never give her brother a chance. Now it looked as if they had made it to a fresh start.

Moving closer, so he could see them through the doorway, he smiled at the backs of their heads. Tori knelt in front of the bench and Brian leaned over, watching her go over the machine's parts in a quiet tone. Clearing his throat, he asked if anyone were hungry, getting a loud affirmative from both parties.

Laying the tools down, they made their way over to the large sink in the back corner to clean the grease off their hands before going into the house. Tori locked the garage for the night, and smiled at the smell of the delicious food when she opened the front door to their tiny cottage.

Brian put the plates on the table and the three of them sat to enjoy a peaceful meal together for the first time since she had returned home. He felt so ecstatic at her newfound acceptance of him, he could not seem to stop talking, and chattered on about his past motorcycle experience, which wasn't much.

Michael joined in the conversation, and the three of them vocalized about different types of bikes, makes and models, and which one would be good for Brian, should he choose to learn to ride. He seemed a little leery on the subject, "I hate to admit it, but I don't have much in the way of coordination. I guess I'm afraid I'll crash or something. I mean, I grew up on a farm and I don't even like to ride horses!"

Tori took the opportunity to laugh at him, reassuring him that he had nothing to fear. "I could teach you, ya know," she made the offer, genuinely hoping he would accept. It felt strange to her, having him in her life. They had agreed for him to stay for a month, but she wondered how it would work out, as she didn't have a strong track record for keeping deadlines.

The possibility he would stay in the small town and never return to his fame and fortune flittered through her mind. Considering this for a moment, she knew there would only be a slim chance if any of that happening. *I'm sure he'll eventually know what he's here to learn and be ready to reclaim his place in the band.*

Another idea crossed her mind, and it saddened her a little. *He might want me to go home with him.* Looking across the table at her husband, she became fully aware that this truly was the life she wanted to lead, no more, no less. *If Brian wants to know me, it'll be here. This small town is my home, and I have no desire to taste the life of glamour he has learned to languish in.*

Smiling at their conversation, Tori pushed the thoughts from her mind. She had learned to live in the moment, to cherish the time she had with people, and this would be her first taste of what real family is all about. She didn't want to waste a single minute of it worrying about the past... or the future.

Sending her brother to bed early, she informed him she would be up at 5:00 am if he cared to join her run.

Brian gave her an odd look, not able to recall the last time he had awoken at such an ungodly hour. It would be more likely he would have still been up at 5:00 am back home, partying or getting laid. Trying to be polite, he chose not to share his evaluation of her idea, only nodding and saying he would consider it when he got up the next morning.

Tori smiled, surmising he would pass when the time came, as she felt pretty sure he was a *'you only live once'* kind of guy under normal circumstance. Taking her husband into their chamber, she could feel her heart rate quicken, her breathing becoming erratic with the thought of what lay in store.

She and Michael made love every time their heads hit the pillow. Understanding her heavy desire for sex, he did his best to keep up with her. He never attempted to get nasty with her, and she would sometimes imagine making the move for herself, taking him into the realm of dirty fucking he had once told her matter-of-factly that he was not into.

Dismissing the idea, she felt compelled to keep things as they were, a firm division between the man she loved and would spend her life with, and the darkness of her life that her time with Enrique had represented. She thought about him occasionally, and his number remained in her wallet. *I know if I ever need him, I can reach him, but for now, this is where I belong.*

She made slow progress at undressing her lover, her hands working their magic as they removed his clothing to find the flesh below. She loved to kiss and caress his finely toned muscles, and the feel of his fingers gliding across hers brought her desire screaming to the surface.

Dropping her shirt onto the growing pile of garments, Michael could feel the fire building within him. Removing her jeans, he pushed her back and buried his face in the trimmed hairs that covered her soft folds, locating her pleasure center and working it freely with his tongue and teeth. He loved the way she panted when he did this, driving him to the edge.

He finished her expertly, and she lay trembling on the edge of the bed, her legs hanging off the side as he knelt between them, running his hands up and down her silky smooth limbs. Squeezing the muscles as they twitched, he became overcome with a singular idea.

Standing, he rolled her over onto her knees, so that she knelt on the edge of the bed, her body in the perfect position as he stood behind her. Pushing himself inside her soft folds, he grasped her hips and began to slam his body against her in hard quick thrusts. She gasped in surprise by his choice of position, it being something the two of them had never shared.

Looking down, he could see her round, crinkled orifice, allowing his thumb to slide lightly across it, causing it to pulse as he teased the delicate skin. Grasping her hip again, he slapped against her, not shifting to the new location, but allowing her to consider that he might. *You know she wants you to*, the thought tore at him as he pushed his body against hers.

He took her hard and fast until he became exhausted and he finished himself loudly, obviously enjoying the change in their routine. Stretching across the bed together, they lay sprawled over it, panting. Her back still to him, he used his fingers to feel her swollen cleft that dripped with her juices mixed with his own.

Transferring the thick ooze with a sliding motion, he used his right hand to wet the rounded fold of her and allowed his fingers to toy with her, the muscles pulsing as his thumb slipped inside. She made small noises as he teased her, reaching back to catch his palm with her trembling digits. She held him stopped in place, but did not push him away, and he wondered if she really wanted him to take her that way.

The thought pained him again, and he promised himself he would never do that to her. He loved this woman and felt that doing so would be a show of great disrespect. *If that's really how she wants to be treated, she should go back to the dark haired man who loved to fuck her in that degrading manner.*

Kissing and nuzzling the back of her neck, he whispered to her quietly, "You know I will never do that to you." His left hand pushed deep into the black curls, caressing her scalp tenderly as he spoke. He could hear her gentle sobs and feel her ragged breath.

Tori felt torn, between the two worlds again, not sure where her loyalties really lay. Cursing to herself, she knew she only wanted him to feel that she loved him, which she did, but her indecision had been exposed and she felt dirty all over again, unworthy of his devotion. Pushing his fingers out of their new location, she freed herself enough to roll away from him, turning to look him in the eye as she confessed her sins.

True Desire

"I'm so sorry," she whispered into the dim light. She could make out his face clearly in the grey moon glow that filtered in through the window. "I just have this thing inside of me; I don't really know what to do about it."

Michael reached out, smoothing the hair away from her face so he could peer into her eyes more easily. He didn't have to say he understood; she knew that he did. "You have a plan?" he asked in his sultry tone. Inwardly, he smiled to himself, *she always has a plan.*

"I want to be here," she countered eagerly. "I want to love you. I know this is where I belong." She spoke hoarsely, the emotion causing her voice to crackle.

Michael lay quiet for a moment, mulling over her choice of words. *She's such a smart lady, such strong intuition about how the heart and mind are connected.* The hard part could be found in the words she didn't say. She had said what she thought in her head, but she didn't mention her real desires, the ones that come from the heart. Many people allow them to be the guiding force in their lives.

Not Tori. She's too smart for that. She feels that hearts are easily deceived, and it's only by clear thought and understanding that a true path should be chosen. Nodding, Michael leaned forward and kissed her pretty lips. His heart skipped a beat in reaction, and he knew that he loved her more than ever.

Pushing her onto her back, he split her legs to reclaim her. She accepted him eagerly, and he continued to whisper to her as he moved gently in slow, deep strokes. "You are so perfect for me. They thought they made you for their terrible purpose. But that's not really what you are for."

He stared into her crystal blue eyes beneath him, continuing to run his fingers through her hair. "You were made for me... to lay beside me in the dark... to walk beside me in the light. The perfect woman to share my life. Nothing to hide, nothing to fear. Completely free to be ourselves in all that we are and do."

Her lip trembled at his words, knowing they were correct. Wrapping her legs around him tightly, she held him inside her while he moved within her sloppy wetness. Her heart brimming, she knew he spoke the truth. No man had ever touched her heart the way he had. Not Enrique, not Brett, and certainly not Eli.

Grasping her limbs behind the knee, she pulled them down and back, allowing him fuller access to her warmth and he could drive himself against her more heavily, causing her to moan loudly. She could feel the liquid running between her folds to coat the other place, the one other men used; men who did not love her like Michael did. This was right and he was right, and she knew that in time she would lose the old desires if she left them where they lay, clinging to the truth in her life.

When they were satiated, the couple turned to snuggle beneath their light summer blankets, content to hold each other in the darkness until sleep overtook them. The alarm rang out at 5:00 am, and Tori sprang up to go for her morning routine.

Michael rolled over, gratified to stretch across the

warm spot in the bedding that she left behind, and she smiled as she ran her fingers playfully through his brown curls.

Briefly, she thought of rousing him to satisfy her physical needs. Instead, she dressed in her black spandex and slipped out of the house in the early morning darkness. Making her way through her warm up run, she returned to her tree and made it through twelve sets of twelve, pushups, squats, lunges and speed skaters. *God, I love this place, the coolness of the air. Fall will be here soon, and the first anniversary of our second meeting.*

Leaning against her tree, she thought about how hard she had always pushed herself to remain physically fit. *The Scorpions are gone. I think I might be ready to take on a more traditional role as a woman; as much as I am able.*

Staring out into the early light, Tori allowed her mind to wander. *It's time for me to see a doctor. I need to know once and for all what my future can and cannot hold.* If Eddie had successfully ruined her chances of ever bearing a child, so be it, but she needed to know for sure so she could plan the path before her accordingly.

Taking to relaxing stretches, she considered the role her brother could possibly have in her changing life. *We have reached an agreement, I guess; and I understand it has benefits for me. I love to empty my heart and soul into my music.* Even though Michael had wanted her to write happy songs, she found the best were the ones where she delved into the deepest darkest memories and pain of her life.

Brian could help her reach into that void more fully, making it possible for her to record the music on paper. *That way my words have the sound that brings them to life.* She never intended to share her music with the world, but writing it down still had a certain appeal. *They say our paths are crossed by people for a reason. Maybe this is why my brother has been returned to my life, even if I wanted to avoid it.*

Feeling relaxed, Tori made her way into the house. Removing eggs and bacon from the refrigerator, she placed a large flat griddle across two of the burners on the stove. Cracking open eggs, she began to scramble them, strips of meat frying on the far end. Adding a small amount of cheese and seasoning, she stirred the mixture to the proper consistency and started a pot of coffee.

Awakening to the smell of the delicious breakfast, both of the men in her life soon appeared. Brian wore a horrid case of bed-head, his dark locks sticking out straight in several places. She laughed inwardly, the smile teasing her lips. *He's so not a morning person, like Lins.* Only allowing herself a brief moment to think about the girl who had helped her so much, she soon pushed the thoughts away and returned to the present.

Taking their seats, the trio ate merrily and made plans for the day. "I think I'll take you through the next set of repairs on the bike," Tori put her hat in the ring.

"Not today," Brian challenged. "Today, I'm in charge. We can start by playing together, find out what you really know, and go from there."

Remembering her promise and her morning of brainstorming, she nodded her agreement to the agenda.

"Hey, that's a great idea," Michael quickly agreed, "It'll give me a chance to take care of some business in town that I've been neglecting."

His wife eyed him, slightly suspicious before giving him a small grin, confident he once again had something up his sleeve, and he let himself out of the house shortly thereafter to be on his way, planning his next big surprise for the love of his life.

Arriving at the massive Victorian style house, Michael stood on the porch and surveyed his accomplishments thus far. Reaching up, he gave a light tap on the frame before opening the screen and calling inside, "Hello?" He heard Marge reciprocate from upstairs, and made his way into the living room, allowing the door to close gently behind him.

Straightening up a bit, he felt comfortable in the house, as he and Marge had formed a strange type of friendship in the last few weeks. *She's in worse shape than she lets on; I really hate that I'm not allowed to tell anyone how much she really hurts or how little she's able to do on a daily basis.* He had reluctantly agreed, on the stipulation that she would keep his wife's past a secret, and accept their help.

He had been watching Tori's softer side grow during the spring as she had worked with the woman's grandsons. He knew she would benefit from helping the older woman, and intended for Tori to accompany him on his visits. Marge had been slow to approve of his being there, but eventually had come to appreciate the younger man's aid.

Coming down the stairs, she could see her sandy-haired benefactor putting things in order. She gave him a small smile, "I hear yur wife's returned. I take it our town is once again safe frum th' hoodlums who would overrun us?"

"Damn, you heard my good news. I knew I should have told you sooner." He liked her sense of humor and agreed with a laugh, "Yes ma'am, our town is safe. Things are complicated though. Her brother is still here, not leaving for a few more weeks. I'll start bringing her with me when that time comes, if you don't mind, so she can help out with some of the chores around here."

She nodded slightly, "Are you sure she'll wanna come help a mean ol' woman like me?"

He bobbed his head reassuringly, knowing his wife's good nature would surely prevail. He set about taking care of the things that would need doing around the old place, humming to himself while he worked.

What Rivalry?

Tori grabbed a quick shower, while Brian set about cleaning up the kitchen. When she returned, they worked easily together, talking about likes and dislikes, making a comparison between the two of them. She had begun to make a list of the things that they had in common, and found it especially gratifying that they both held such a deep appreciation for music and played the guitar, among other things.

She liked the fact that they both spoke French, and using it often had made it a goal to help him regain full use of the language. Deep down, she feared her having spoken it to be one of the reasons Eddie had chosen her for his sinister plot.

Finishing with the chores, they climbed into her pickup to take the television over and tossed it into the metal building with the rest of the group's instruments. Tori felt glad to be rid of it, as she saw no need for such a device.

Bringing his guitar and amp out of his bedroom, they shifted things around in the front room to allow for everything to be set up. The space had begun to feel a little cramped, but still held the necessary items to maintain its functionality if they were going to play together without moving back out to the garage.

Taking up their instruments, they quickly went through what the girl knew, and it did not take Brian long to solidify his belief that she was truly talented. Listening and watching her hands and expression, she played one riff after another, and he grasped that she played from within. He brought out several pieces of sheet music, and then discovered that she had no clue how to read it.

"But, they had music in the store, in Terry's shop in LA. You never even looked at it?" he asked in a disbelieving tone.

Slightly embarrassed, she admitted, "I never cared about it. Henry taught me how to play on his six string in Brazil, and all I had was my ear to go by. When I picked up the electric model last year, I used what I already knew. I felt good when I played, and I made it reflect what I felt inside."

She grinned as she confessed, "I loved that white guitar, and a few times even discouraged people from buying it so I could keep it there. I even played music on the speakers during the day to try it out for myself when I was alone."

Running his fingers through his hair, he decided he might as well start at the beginning, with the treble clef, the ledger lines, and what the notes and rests look like. He found that she was a quick study, absorbing everything he told her like a sponge. She brought out a spiral notebook, and made notes periodically about the things that he said, intending to study and reflect upon them later.

He also took the time to show her how to properly record the chords she used, which is what she had more or less been trying to do with her previous attempts to put her thoughts into written form. Brian smiled at her overjoyed expression, as she would be able to take some of the first few songs she had written and turn what had been in her mind into something he could read and follow.

Michael returned in the early evening to discover they had begun playing together, and she sang to him while playing one of her most-beloved pieces. Entering the house, he felt a small stab of disappointment that she chose to start with one of her saddest songs, *not that there are any happy ones in her notebook, either... only degrees of sorrow,* he grimaced.

Allowing them to continue, Michael prepared their meal of baked chicken, vegetables and salad. He rather enjoyed seeing the two of them, playing side by side, and noted they appeared quite happy to do so.

Giving her brother a wide grin, Tori's fingers moved through a complex riff.

Brian's brow furrowed with a small twinge of jealousy. *She's only been playing a short time. What has taken me years to perfect, she seems to have come by naturally.* "You know, that was always a problem between us," he pointed back and forth at her and himself with his thumb, "The way you make everything look so simple."

"And what's that supposed to mean?" her jaw tightened.

"You were always so... perfect." He could not think of a better word to use than that. "I always worked hard and struggled. You," he indicated her with an open palm, "You always had *everything* easy. People liked you and you always got your way. You learned everything like on the first try and never had to work for anything."

Tori stared at him, still not fully grasping the meaning of what he said. "I do too work hard. I work hard every day." She felt angry, as if he had called her lazy or something.

Shaking his head, he tried to clarify. "That's not what I meant. I didn't say you *don't* work hard, I said you didn't *have* to. There's a difference. You put yourself into things because you want to, but even if you don't, you're ok. Me, if

I hadn't pushed myself, I never would've been able to play in the band."

She stared at him, a strange feeling in the pit of her stomach. *Does he really think I'm good at this?* Laughing at him, "Stop picking on me like that. I'm not stupid enough to think I'm any better than the average person, much less as good as you are." Inwardly, she beamed with joy.

Brian let the subject go, only to return to it over dinner. Commenting in an offhand manner, he made a bold suggestion, "The two of you should come with me to New York. You could play with the band and give that a try. I think you have totally missed my point about your ability, and I would really like the rest of the guys to back me up on this. I'm sure that they would, too."

Michael's head snapped up at the remark, giving his newly found brother-in-law a long stare. He had wanted the two of them to get to know each other, but he had no intention of allowing her to head off after him, delving into the dirty lifestyle he had witnessed that the band enjoyed. Thinking about the tall white house he currently worked to secure for them, he knew it would be imperative that they *not* follow that suggestion.

Chuckling quietly, he tried to cover his concern and guide the conversation in a more suitable direction. "She don't wanna go hang out with a bunch of rowdy guys, drinking and carousing at all hours of the day and night." He made the observation flippantly and then ploughed on with local news.

"School starts next Monday and Trish wanted to know if the boys would be welcome here again this year." He gave his wife an encouraging smile as she considered how she would feel about having the pair around again.

Tori hid her guilty thoughts, seeing her mate's eager expression. Playing with Brian had awakened a new desire inside of her, and she had experienced a brief flicker of excitement at the idea of playing with her brother's band. "I'm not really sure the boys will like that. They haven't even spoken to me since I got back, and I'm really concerned about what they have heard about me since we were publicly escorted out of town by the Feds back in June."

It was a genuine concern, and even as Trish might have been firmly on Tori's side, there were others in town that were not so willing to accept her back after the unpleasant departure. He nodded, "I'll have a word with the boys and see if I can get to the bottom of things."

Tori mumbled a small agreement. In her heart, the anxiety lingered, *I don't really want to be tied down to such a commitment.* She refused to vocalize her distress, only flipping her gaze between the two men as she considered where each of their suggestions might lead, and the desire to be able to choose.

Being mid-August, still summer for all intents and purposes, the three made their way outside to relax on the grass under Tori's tree after dinner. The sun sank low in the sky, the sound of the locusts buzzing in the limbs above them. Hearing the hum of mosquitos, Michael went back inside, returning a few minutes later with a large citronella candle, and placing it in the midst of the group.

Watching the flicker of the small fire, Tori felt compelled to share one of her tales about her life with her brother. "So, are you up for hearing a story?"

"A story?" he sounded shocked, "Is it going to be gruesome or depressing?" He hated to have the fine evening ruined.

Giving him a devious smile, "No, it isn't. I was about twelve or thirteen, which is before the gruesome and depressing stuff really started."

Brian nodded, "I guess, go for it," inwardly eager to

hear something from her past in her own words.

She began wistfully, "The camp I grew up in was a beautiful place, but wild in every sense of the word."

"Wild, huh, like with Lions and Tigers and Bears, Oh my?" Brian mocked her slightly, and Tori only stared at him, not understanding the reference.

"No, it's South America, not Africa; there weren't any of those things," her voice trailed away in her confusion.

Grinning even more, he shook his head, "Never mind, sis; it's a joke, but it's not funny if I have to explain it. Well, actually it is, 'cause you have no clue what I'm talking about." He laughed out loud, Michael joining him for a moment.

Tori smiled to herself, feeling only slightly put out that they were making fun of her lack of common knowledge. "Ok, well someday, you're gonna have to explain that one to me. But, as it were, we lived in a beautiful rainforest, which had a small cabin in the center where we prepared meals and supplies were stored, along with my wall of books."

"There were four of the Dragons who stayed with me all the time. Henry, Michael's brother, was my full-time caretaker, always looking after me, but there were also three others. The rest of the Dragons had left for a few months and would return later in the year, when the seasons changed."

Shifting, she stretched out her legs and continued, "I was getting old enough, and the group had begun to teach me more about grown up things, such as building a fire, hunting and preparing food. This was the first time they took me anaconda hunting. I was only about five foot tall, but they agreed it would be safe for me to be out and about without too much risk of being seen as prey by larger snakes."

"Holy shit," Brian's eyes grew wide, "You mean snakes would come after you? Like, chase you?"

It was Tori's turn to laugh, "I told you, it was a jungle.

Yeah, I learned right away that we only stayed on top of the food chain if we were smart. Danger always lay around us."

"So anyways, we had sticks that we used when we hunted, and they taught me how to fashion a set for myself. Carrying the sticks, we went down to the water that ran along the western side of our property. The trees there were massive, hanging over the dirty water in huge arches." Her eyes held a distant glaze as she described it.

"Along the water's edge, there lived a large den of capybara, which we ate fairly often." Seeing his confused grimace, she elaborated, "A capybara is basically a large rat, so to speak, being in the rodent family. They live in small groups, but sometimes larger numbers. Anacondas love to eat them, so they made good bait for the snakes."

"Using the sticks and a machete, we would capture and kill the longer serpents, anywhere from five feet and up, preferring to pass if they were less than five feet long. I had never been with them on a hunt before, and found it a thrilling event, the only drawback being the bugs." She giggled at how the mosquitos had triggered the happy memory.

Michael laughed too, remembering the rattlesnake she had made it look so easy to acquire. "A skill to last a lifetime," he teased.

"Of course, but anacondas don't have venom, so there's a lot less danger in that respect. And if you use your stick properly and don't piss them off, they are rather docile creatures. Fast little suckers too. Did you know they can live for months on one good meal? Amazing really." She still had a faraway expression on her face as her voice trailed away.

Relieved, Brian spouted, "I thought your life was terrible before you were found." He gave Michael a scowl, having been told how she had been raped and regularly beaten.

"That was after I joined the group. When I was young, things were different. They treated me well for the most part, except that I was alone, with no other children around, and I really didn't understand things. It wasn't so bad, it just wasn't normal." Tori looked at the ground for a moment, feeling conflicted about her childhood.

Brian nodded slowly, "Yeah, after the accident, my life changed, too. I moved to grandma and grandpa's farm permanently, and lived there about nine years before grandma died. She had been sick a long time though. Even when you were still around, she wasn't doing well, so it was amazing she lasted that long." He paused for a moment of reflection and she gave him a small grin.

"I had really gotten into my guitar and wanted to go make music with the group, but grandpa didn't want me to go. Said he needed my help on the farm. Then he got sick and died unexpectedly a short time after her, and I was suddenly free."

His face drawn into a frown, Tori asked, "Weren't you happy then? Because you really don't look like it."

Brian shrugged, "It turned out to be a lot more work than I thought it would be, and after that, I basically had no family left to speak of. A few aunts and uncles, some cousins, but I haven't seen or heard from any of them since grandpa's funeral."

He flopped his hands in a more exaggerated manner. "I guess I got to where I kept people away from me. Kinda hard to know who to trust, much less not wanting to care about someone I would eventually lose."

Tori nodded; she knew exactly what he meant.

Looking over at her husband, she had a familiar stab of pain and fear of losing what little she had. She loved him and hoped he knew how precious he was to her. Reaching, she ran the backs of her fingers along his denim covered leg that lay stretched out beside her own.

Speaking softly, "We have a lot in common, don't we. I'm glad we got this chance to know each other. I'm sure our lives won't ever be close, but hopefully you'll make time to visit me down the road." She smiled, having effectively dismissed his idea of going with him to New York when he left. She knew Michael wouldn't want her there, and she wasn't about to let him down if she could help it.

The night closed in around them, and they put the candle out as they made their way inside. Brian wasn't ready to give up on his idea of taking her home with him, so he didn't comment on her final observation, allowing the couple to go to bed in peace.

Safely inside their room, Michael put his hands on his wife as soon as the door had been shut. He loved the way she felt and always yielded to his touch, eager to please him. Kissing her deeply, he ran his hands over her body before he began to remove her clothing. She smiled widely at him, returning the caresses.

Their hunger building, they undressed in a playful silence, kicking off boots and lifting shirts over their heads. Running her fingers through the hairs that camouflaged her name, she felt a gleeful twist in her stomach, knowing he loved her so much.

Kissing her again, his hands raked over her while removing her clothing and dropping it on the floor. Guiding her over to the bed, he lay her down, kissing bare skin along her torso as his face slid down towards the warm folds that he so dearly adored toying with.

Michael, thrilled by the taste of her, ran his fingers across her hairs and listening to the gentle pants the movement produced. She had learned to trust him at this, and he recalled how hard it had been for her to endure on their wedding day.

INDELIBLE

Tonight she felt eager, knowing he would put her over the edge, giving her that feeling that sapped her strength and satisfied her desire like no other man ever had or could.

Painful Truth

The following morning, Tori made an appointment to see a doctor, his office located in a nearby town. She felt nervous, having never experienced a real gynecological exam before. Fortunately, it was a small practice, so she got in before the end of the week.

The morning of the appointment, she dressed early, leaving a note on the table that she would be back after lunch, and left the house before either of the two men were awake. She wasn't willing to share her thoughts with her husband, wanting to spare his feelings. *No sense getting his hopes up if it's really not an option; I'll tell him when I know something concrete.*

Stopping by the diner to visit with Trish, she saw the older woman smile as she pushed through the glass door. Her eyes were warm, but she hung back slightly, so the girl took a seat at the short counter and laid it on the line, "Why is everyone acting so funny around me?"

Trish's expression changed to surprise, "Well, hun; we aren't really sure if you're ready, I guess."

"Ready," Tori appeared thoughtful for a moment, *ready for what?*

Seeing her troubled eyes, her friend continued, "Ya know, Michael loves you. He did his best t' explain why you was picked up by those detectives and how you had been hiding here. He was tryin' t' protect you and not tell things you wouldn't want everyone t' know, so that left a lot o' room for those with loose tongues t' make up a story they wanted t' tell."

Tori stared at her, grasping her meaning. *People have been talking and the things they're saying aren't nice, and more than likely false.* The saddest part, they are probably things not nearly as bad as the painful truth. Nodding slowly, she spoke in a loud whisper, "Well then, I guess it's time I set the record straight if I plan on staying here."

"You don't have t' explain anything t' me," Trish gave her friend an encouraging shake of her head. "I've been around a long time, an' I know th' look o' needing a new life when I see it. You don' owe these other yahoos any explanation either. You just go on, bein' who you are, an' it'll all take care o' itself." She had placed her hand on top of the girl's and gave it an affectionate squeeze.

Tori felt better as she looked into the bright green eyes of her best friend. Managing a small smile, she inquired about the boys. "So, they'll be coming over next week after school then?"

"Yeah," Trish agreed, "But it may take a few days for Chris t' feel comfortable again, havin' heard some o' the stories, but it'll work out."

Tori only nodded, checking the time and deciding to go. She trotted out to her pickup, glad she had made the effort to check in with the diner's owner. *That woman has her finger on the pulse of the town and knows what's going on,* she grinned sheepishly. *There are at least a few people who care about me still around.*

It took about half an hour for her to arrive at the medical facility. Inside, Tori could feel the butterflies in her stomach. A cheerful place, the walls were painted mint green with bright pink accents. The girl at the front desk wore her honey colored hair swept up into a bun, with perky red lipstick and nails. Studying them as the girl wrote with a ballpoint pen, Tori considered the manicure session she had shared with Sharon and Lins back in LA, the memory causing her to shudder.

Holding out a clipboard, the girl instructed, "Take the little sticker and place it on the tube after you put your urine sample into it in the bathroom. Then, fill out the paperwork and return it to the counter." The girl chewed her gum noisily while she spoke. "Any questions?" she asked in a tone that made Tori uncomfortable; she refrained from making any queries, deciding she would figure it out.

Laying the clipboard on a pink upholstered chair, she went through the entry labeled *restroom* and closed the door. Snapping the lock, she looked around and noticed a detailed list of directions on the wall for her to follow.

Taking one of the paper cups, she filled it while she sat on the toilet, and then transferred the warm liquid into one of the small tubes. Attaching the sticker that contained her name to the tube, she placed it in the rack that sat in the pass through, presumably so the lab could get it from the other side, and slid the door closed. Finally, washing her hands, she exited the small room.

Inhaling deeply, she gave herself a pep-talk. *You're ok, baby girl; this is something you need to do.* Lifting the board, Tori took the seat and began to go over the forms. She quickly realized she had no idea what her family history held, and her own sketchy at best. Providing what little she could, she took the items to the counter, and the girl scowled at the lack of information that had been given.

"I also need your insurance card," the lively red lips snapped.

Tori shrugged, "I don't have insurance; I'll pay cash

for whatever the bill is."

The girl gave her a dubious glare as she indicated for her to sit again and wait to be called.

The chilled air in the waiting area left her glad that she wore her leather jacket, an accessory she seldom went without. Flipping through a few magazines, Tori crossed her legs and bounced her foot nervously.

Inspecting her wedding band, she thought about Michael's message to her hidden inside. The memory of the day he gave it to her came flooding back to her, and she smiled, hoping the doctor would have good news for them and their plans for the future would be bright.

After what seemed like an eternity, a nurse in hot pink scrubs opened a wide door and indicated Tori should follow her. Leading her into the back, she said, "Go ahead an' take off yur jacket hun, le's get a good weight on you." Tori noticed her inspecting her scarred arms as she took her blood pressure and recorded her height on the paperwork.

Next, the woman led her down a narrow hallway to a room containing an odd bench in the center and a chair in the corner, a curtain hanging next to it. Handing her a sheet, she commanded "Take off all yur clothes an' sit on th' table. Cover yourself with this, an' th' doctor'll be in shortly."

Left alone, Tori unfolded the wrap. Frowning, she thought of her days in the bush camp, when Tony had tended to her while she sat naked in front of God and everyone. *I guess other women must be a great deal more self-conscious than I am.*

Kicking off her boots and doing as instructed, she climbed onto the table wrapped in the fabric. Considering her past life, she would have passed on the uncomfortable cloth. *This damn thing should've been about two foot larger than it is. But, the doctor might find me sitting buck naked out of line, so I guess I'll do my best to comply.*

Waiting long enough for boredom to set in, Tori's eyes scanned the room impatiently. The entry lay to her left, and straight across the small dressing area with a hanging curtain. The remainder of the wall held cabinets, which Tori might have been curious about, but not enough to investigate in her sheet covered condition.

The narrow table she perched on had been topped with paper that crinkled when she moved, and flanked on both sides by large machines against the wall at the head end. She noticed one of them had a monitor on it, with a keyboard below. Leaning over, she inspected it more closely without leaving her perch.

There were also charts and books littering the counter, adorned with pictures of female reproductive organs and the things that can go wrong with them; a truly unnerving sight for someone in her condition. She looked over what she could see from her vantage point, waiting for the door to open so they could get on with it.

A short time later, there came a small rap on the door, and a middle-aged man with the beginnings of grey in his dark hair entered, followed by another young girl who carried a laptop. He smiled as their eyes met, and Tori gave him a small grin.

She again felt self-conscious of the markings that covered her body as he offered his hand, which she managed to give a limp shake. He instructed her to lie down on the table so he could examine her breasts.

Feeling them briefly through the thin material, he moved back to the foot end of the table, asking her to place one foot in each stirrup and slide down so that her rear end rested in the proper position. Unexplainably, Tori's heart began to pound. *Relax*, she clenched her fists, *you've been seen and touched by lots of men*, but this was a whole different experience, with much more at stake.

Covered in latex gloves, his fingers felt cold as they touched her female parts. He continued to explain the process in a soothing tone while he took a sample for the lab and dropped it in a small jar. Closing the lid, he placed it on the counter next to the literature. He then slid a few of his digits inside her and pressed down on her lower abdomen, making observations to the girl who busily typed notes using her small computer.

Not able to see everything fully, Tori breathed deeply as the exam continued, occasionally feeling a stab of pain that caused her to inhale sharply. Beginning to tremble, either from the coldness of the air or the uncertainty of the events taking place, she struggled to remain in control.

Finally, removing the stretchy coverings, the doctor tossed them into the wastebasket while giving her permission to sit up. Leaning his rear end against the counter facing her, he studied her for a moment and then commented, "I'm curious about your history; your information here is almost blank. Do you have any previous records that I might go over?"

Thinking briefly about Dr. Bennet and his medical examination, she shook her head and lifted her chin to reply, "Not that I would trust. I've never really seen doctors before."

He smiled slightly and stood thinking for a moment.

Tori played with her fingers in her lap, the sheet clutched about her and anxiety beginning to show as she stared at him with wide eyes.

"If there aren't any records," he opened is palm towards her, "Is there anything in your past *you* feel might be relevant here? Any kind of trauma, accidents, anything? You listed a prior pregnancy," he glanced over at her chart, "But zero live births. I feel as if I need to know some details about that."

Tori looked at her hands, bouncing her feet slightly as she considered how to reply. Giving him a slow nod, she pursed her lips, "I was raised by a group of men," she explained briefly. "I had a pretty normal childhood, but after my periods came, I was abused physically... sexually..."

She broke off, picking at her nails as she recalled her induction. "One of them gave me an abortion, with a clothes hanger, about six years ago. He wanted to keep me from ever getting pregnant again. That's why I'm here really; I want to know if it's true, and if it can be fixed."

Nodding, he asked for more, "And what're your periods like?"

"After the procedure, I only get a bit of spotting. Pretty unpredictable really." Looking hopeful, she added, "But back when I started getting them, you know, for the couple of years before the abortion, they came every twenty-eight days, lasted four, and I could set a calendar by them."

The doctor raised an eyebrow in surprise, "Couple of years? It says here you're twenty-five years old." He did some quick math with his fingers, "That puts you at, what, around seventeen at your menarche? That's very late. They didn't take you to a doctor then?"

Tori shook her head, not really sure what he meant. She had begun to regret her choice to see him, as he made her feel very wrong about herself. Seeing that he waited for an actual answer, she conceded, "I don't know what that means, *menarche*. There had been some concern about my puberty coming late, but no doctor." She didn't want to go into details about where and how she had grown up, already put out by what she had shared.

He stared at her a moment, "It just means your first menstruation," he wafted the air absently. He pinched his lip, "Do you work out?" His question seemed out of place with the prior conversation.

"I work out every day - " she cut her reply short when his jaw dropped slightly.

"And when did you begin this routine?" he sounded even more cryptic.

"Since I was about five," she continued to cooperate half-heartedly.

A long "Ahh," escaped him as he made the connection, "I get it."

"Get dressed," he directed, "And I'll meet you in my office in a few minutes to discuss your case." Turning to the girl, they exited the small room, with him giving her instructions as they walked.

Putting on her panties, Tori felt an odd, nervous excitement, knowing she would finally have the truth about her condition and her chances of ever carrying Michael's child. She had never allowed herself to dream or even hope that she would, but physically being there, she had to admit, the thought of doing so left her breathless.

Sliding her jacket on while leaving the cramped room, she pulled her hair free, and the girl outside directed her to another chamber at the end of the hall. Inside, the doctor's wide desk was strewn with papers. Taking one of the chairs across from it, she noticed the large diplomas hanging on the wall, proclaiming Donald Lazenby had graduated with honors.

Almost as soon as she sat down, the doctor came in, giving her a warm smile and shaking her hand for a proper introduction. A friendly sort, Tori briefly compared him to Dr. Carlisle, who had spent many hours with her at the mental hospital before she had been released.

"There is a doctor that I saw, more in a mental health capacity, who might have some useful information for you," she began quietly.

"That won't be necessary," he waved his hand, "I have

what I need really; I was only curious how long your history had been documented. You will be an interesting case, I think," he smiled as he spoke to her.

"I believe you may have scar tissue, inside your uterus." Holding out a palm towards the ceiling, he poked the open hand with a finger from the other, "Asherman's Syndrome it's called, but it's something that can be fixed. However, I'm more concerned about your late onset of menses, and it may be related to your heavy exercise. This leads to other problems that can be dangerous for you. We need to do more tests to be sure everything is ok. After that, we can talk about the repairs to your reproductive organs."

Taking a brief pause to lean back in his chair, his tone dropped as he continued, "My receptionist tells me you are a cash patient. I want to warn you before you make any decisions, that everything will need to be paid up front, and it can be expensive. Also, you will need about two weeks of recovery time if and when we are able to do your procedure, as we will be placing a balloon inside while your body heals."

Tori looked down at the desk, "Anything else I should know?" She asked the question absently, knowing she would have to do a bit of soul-searching before she took the next step. She felt a little deflated, as the path ahead would not be as easy as she had hoped it would be.

"I can give you some pamphlets, or you can look it up online." He reached over, handing her a folded brochure after writing a small note along the side. "Right now, I'm sending you over to have a bone density scan, and I also want to have some blood drawn for testing. Have you eaten anything this morning?"

"No, I got up to come straight over," she explained, "So I didn't have time."

"That's fortunate," he agreed, "We can do a fasting

blood work up."

Tori didn't really see any of it as fortunate, but she didn't bother to argue, taking the slip of paper from him for the tests. "How will I get the results?"

"My receptionist will make an appointment for next week." Rising, he showed her into the hallway. Leading her around the corner, he dropped her off at the lab, where they drew her blood.

Ready to exit the building, Tori stopped to check out and inquired how much everything he had spoken of would cost. At hearing the sum, she felt a bit shocked at the price tag. *Albeit, we do have a large amount of money in the bank, but this will be quite a chunk, and not something we can spend without some consideration.*

Paying the bill in cash, she then set an appointment for her results. Leaving the office, she walked the three blocks to the testing facility for the bone density scan, allowing herself to prepare for more prodding. By the time she had finished, she felt exhausted and desperately wanted to go home.

Driving the short distance, Tori's head swam. *How am I going to approach the subject?* She felt the need to talk to her husband about everything that had transpired that day. *But, I should wait until Brian goes home. I don't really want to involve him. This is something Michael and I will have to decide.*

Pulling up next to the shop, she tossed the pamphlet and paperwork into the glove box. Putting on a smile, she made her way inside to have lunch with her family, saving what needed to be said for another day.

Brotherly Love

Michael had awoken later than normal that morning and made his way out to discover the note his wife had left on the kitchen table. Assuming she was off to talk to someone about a bike, he wadded up the small piece of paper and tossed it in the trash. *Nice, her brother and I get to have a little heart to heart in private.* He had been meaning to speak to him for a few days, and wasn't about to miss the opportunity.

Setting about making coffee and brunch, he took great pains to bang around noisily. After several minutes, he had begun to think he would actually have to beat on the walls to rouse him. Fortunately, the scruffy headed guitar player sauntered in and plunked down in a chair.

"What the hell you makin' all that racket for?" Brian gave the man a disgusted grimace, "Can't you let people get their sleep?"

Michael sneered to himself before he modulated his tone into something on the side of friendly, "Nearly time for lunch, ya' know?" He cut his eyes over at the blue orbs that watched him, eager to get on with their talk before his wife showed up and interrupted them.

Brian tossed his head back, raising his chin to challenge him, "If you say so. Where's sis?"

"Ah, she had some business to handle. Be back in a bit, so I wanted to have lunch ready for her. Nice surprise for her," his mood lightened a little at the thought of taking care of her needs.

Brian watched the back of the older man as he moved, catching the rise in his tone when he spoke about the girl. The man obviously loved her, and he almost felt guilty about his plans. "You know, I really appreciate the way you look after her and all."

Michael snorted a laugh, "Well, thanks, I think; but I don't do it for you." He turned, setting Brian's meal in front of him before he made Tori's plate to place in the oven. "I do it because I care about *her*. And actually, that's something I've been wanting to talk to you about."

Brian speared his green beans warily, the hairs on the back of his neck beginning to bristle, "Oh yeah?"

"Yeah," Michael paused for effect, taking his seat with a plate of his own a few minutes later. "See, Tori is really special to me." Noticing the expression on Brian's face grow dark, he soothed quickly, "And I know you care about her too, don't get me wrong, but she's a lot more fragile than she lets on. She wants us to believe that everything's fine, but really, she needs... you know..." he shrugged, "Special care."

Brian grunted, grinding his teeth for a moment between bites, "How do you figure? She seems pretty self-sufficient to me."

Michael added a dab of ketchup to his plate, taking his time to get to the point. "Yeah, she does, but a lot of that's an act. She doesn't want people to worry about her. Or for her. That's why it's up to us to do what's right by her." He cut his eyes over at the younger man, "That's why I want you to stop suggesting she go to New York with you."

Brian felt as if he'd been slapped, stopping in mid-chew to allow his jaw to hang open briefly, "Are you fuckin' kidding me?"

"No, I'm not kidding you. She has no business there, and you damn well know it." Michael's voice began gaining in volume but remained controlled. "You guys are party out the ass, and she don't need that shit!" He slapped the table with an open palm to emphasize his point.

Brian chewed hastily with his half open mouth, swallowing the bite so he could continue, "And what makes you think you're the one who knows what's best for her? I'm her brother after all – flesh an' blood."

Giving him a cold stare, brown eyes on fire, "Because she's my wife. She chose me and I her. And you'll do what I ask you to do, or you can pack your shit right the fuck now."

Michael's voice still loud, it remained flat calm and Brian could feel his blood run cold, the subtle threat clear. "And if I don't?"

Michael continued picking at his plate, taking a few more bites, and allowing the question to hang in the air. Eventually, he took a sip of his coffee, pushing his plate back to rest his elbows on the table. "If you don't, you won't like how things work out. I know you want to have a relationship with her, and I can agree to that. In fact, I'm all for that. But it's gonna be on my terms."

Leaning back slightly in his chair, he ran his tongue over his teeth, clearing out any leftover debris from his meal. "She'll do what I ask her to do, and if I suggest it's time for you to go, she won't argue with that."

Brian's eyes narrowed, knowing he was on the short end of the stick. "Alright, I promise I won't say anything else about it. But if she wants to go, you're making a mistake by stopping her. Just 'cause you're scared."

"Scared? I'm not scared of anything!"

"Sure you are!" he flung a hand at him, "Scared of

why she chose you. Scared of letting her be who she really is. Scared she might fail – ”

Michael threw up a palm to cut him off, “I *said*, I’m not scared. Alright? So you can save your breath. I am, however, concerned. As I said, she needs taken care of. At least for a while. She doesn’t know much about the world we live in, and you didn’t see where she came from. The things they did to her.”

“Yeah, I know, like the other day, that story she told. Said her childhood was beautiful,” Brian recalled with an annoyed glare.

“No. She said the *place* was beautiful. Her childhood was lonely. And as soon as she was old enough, they took to abusing her, just as I said they did. What the hell do you think she did with the Scorpions?” he glowered at his brother in law. “You think she caught up to them and said, ‘Pretty please, don’t hurt my brother?’ Fuck no. She killed ‘em, man. They’re dead. All of them.”

“She told you that?” Brian’s features twisted in angry disbelief.

“No, she didn’t. She didn’t have to. I know how and why they trained her. I was Special Forces, remember? I know about the dark side of the world we live in, and I watched what they did to her with my own eyes. Trust me, the truth is an ugly thing.”

He stabbed the table with his index finger to drive his point home, “Maybe in a few years, yeah, she can go visit you and play around with you and your friends. But right now, she needs to put down some roots. Solid roots to keep her from going back to that life.”

The front door opened, causing Brian a small jolt of panic. Michael recovered instantly, standing to greet his bride with a wide smile, “There you are!”

The musician stared at him, surprised at how quickly

his tone had changed at the sight of the girl. Pulling out a chair for her, her husband guided her into the seat, "I kept your plate warm for you."

Tori smiled slightly, happy to see her two men sharing a meal and one another's company, even in her absence. "Thanks, I'm glad you guys didn't wait on me. Wasn't sure how long I would be."

"So, did you get it?" his voice cheerful, he pulled the dish out and placed it in front of her.

"Get what?" she stared at him, caught off guard, and confused to think he might have guessed her whereabouts.

"The bike?" he supplied. "Sorry, I assumed from your note you had gone off to check out something special."

A wide grin spread across her features as she thought of the words *something special*. Glancing down at his lips, then back up to his clear brown orbs, she replied calmly, "No, not yet, but I made an offer. We'll have to wait and see how it turns out."

Ashes to Ashes

Feeling the need to supervise the siblings, Michael stayed close to home the next morning. The trio busily worked in the garage, when a black Crown Victoria pulled up in front of the shop. Seeing the shiny hubcaps, they stopped and stared out through the roll-up door. Holding her breath, Tori waited to see who would step out of the car and why.

The engine cut-off, and a tall, thin man exited the vehicle. Relieved it had not been Eli Founder, Tori made her way over to greet Warren La Buff and welcome him to her home, again. He didn't smile as they made their way into the small house in the back.

Taking his previous seat on the couch, La Buff paused before he began, and Tori became afraid he might be there to arrest her. Much to her relief, he appeared angry and started in a bitter tone, "Well, once again, you have escaped the justice you deserve," while opening the large brown packet and withdrawing a thin stack of papers from it.

Holding the first document out to her, he waited for her to read over the form, and Michael fell in beside her to see it as well. Skimming down quickly, Tori could not believe the words. "Is this for real?" she inquired in an airy, high-pitched voice.

"Unfortunately, yes," he stated in his typical condescending manner.

Tori reread the letter again, scarcely able to contain her relief. Basically, it had been addressed to her, thanking her for her recent assistance in the investigation code-named XXXXXXXXXXX. She laughed at seeing the case name crossed out in such a bizarre manner. *However, I'm sure the file is still open, so I understand why it was done. I don't really care, as long as they leave me out of it!*

Further on, it stated that she had been absolved of all activities in connection to the case. Her heart began to pound, knowing they had simply let her go, for the second time. Trying not to get her hopes up, she recalled the way Jim had tried to send her after The Organization. *I hope this isn't just a ploy to try and make that happen.*

"So, what did they do about all the bodies?" she put the question to him anxiously, then gave her husband and brother a sideways look. *Fuck me, I forgot they didn't know what actually happened while I was away.* Neither of them reacted, and she concluded they might have surmised how she had handled the situation.

La Buff only continued his angry glare for a few moments, and then snapped, "The situation was contained. That is all you need to know."

Tori nodded perceptively, satisfied with that response. Seeing that the letter had been officially signed similar to the way her first had been, she knew that it would be legitimate, only for a moment wondering what it would cost her.

Warren looked down at the two papers remaining in his hands as if he were trying to decide which one should be presented next. Making up his mind, he handed her a sheet containing a stamped seal at the bottom. Her eyes making it to the top, it read RECORD OF BIRTH in large bold lettering.

Tori squealed in delight at seeing the page. Her full name, Victoria Nichole Peters, and date of birth, May twenty-first were prominent in the upper portion. The words began to shake as her fingers trembled; *I am no longer Tori Farrell, in any way*. She had been using Anderson since she and Michael were married, but this was different, and she knew it.

The form contained the names of both her parents, and she caught a tear as it slipped from her misty blue orb before it could roll down her cheek. Gazing at Brian, she felt more connected to him, seeing these things in writing, and she anxiously waited to see the last item he had for her.

Having seen the official record, Brian nodded, "I'm curious if Robert Frost had anything to do with this. He's my attorney. We were trying to have your emancipation nullified." Pointing at her birth certificate, he reassured her, "Don't worry, he's a good lawyer. He'll do what he can to see that it gets taken care of properly."

Warren La Buff scowled at the younger man as he handed her the last document; an official court manuscript for a closed session, similar to the one they had held before she left LA. At first, Tori could feel the anger; s*ons of bitches, they convened the committee without me*, but it ebbed as she comprehended what it actually said and what they had done.

Covering her mouth with her left hand, she read the last paragraph aloud:

"By the State of California, the Emancipation of Tori Farrell is hereby nullified. In light of said birth certificate presented on this date, it is accepted that the identity of Victoria Nichole Peters has been verified by DNA analysis and comparison with known sibling, Daniel Brian Peters. She is acknowledged to be alive and well, living under said assumed identity, with an exact age of 25 years, 2 months

and 24 days as of the date of this declaration."

The document had been signed by Special Agent James Godfry, Judge William Carlton, and witnessed by Robert Frost, Attorney at Law.

Hearing the words, Michael and Brian began shouting, while Warren La Buff gave the girl an ice cold stare. He didn't say anything and he didn't have to; this wasn't over if he had his way and Tori hoped he wouldn't.

Standing, La Buff bid them farewell in a gruff tone and marched back to his awaiting ebony chariot. As soon as he had pulled back out on the main highway, he opened his phone, selected a number from the short list and made the call.

A moment later, a male voice picked up on the other end, "Yeah?"

"It's done," La Buff stated.

The voice in the distance emitted a small laugh, "That's good," he boasted.

"How are you going to fix this?" La Buff demanded.

"No worries," his cohort assured him, "It may take some time to arrange, but there is always a way," and the phone disconnected.

Back inside the small house, the celebration continued. After several minutes of laughter and generous hugging, the three returned to the shop. The joyous mood radiated around them as they discussed what should be done next.

Michael pointed out, "Well, you're gonna need to change a few things, love, including getting a driver's license."

Staring at her husband in surprise, she giggled to herself, *he's right! I have proof of my birth; and not that silly emancipation card, either.* Wiping her hands, she announced, "In that case, I'm going to get it today."

Closing up the shop, all three piled into the old brown

pickup. Michael drove and Tori rode between her husband and brother. They were the two people who mattered most in her life, and she could not remember ever being happier.

The test itself went smoothly, as she had been driving the truck for months and had become sufficiently skilled. The paper portion also exceedingly simple, she had her picture snapped wearing a small, elated grin.

Leaving the DPS office, they made their way over to the small social security building to order a replacement card, which took a bit more convincing since she had been dead. Fortunately, they had the nullification letter and the DNA results with which to convince the woman, and were allowed to fill out the proper forms after she made copies of everything.

At last, the group trotted over to a restaurant located within walking distance. They were well ready for a meal after all the excitement, and what the news of the day meant.

"I should go and visit their graves," Tori said quietly as they were seated. "Where're they buried, exactly?" she asked the question timidly, afraid of spoiling the festive atmosphere.

Brian wasn't bothered, happy that she seemed interested in seeing their parents' final resting place. "They're in a little cemetery outside of Harrison, Nebraska. We have a small farm there, in Sioux County." He smiled, and she noted he used the word *we* instead of *I*. His mind tracing over those memories, he wondered what had become of the little girl's body that had been laid to rest beside them.

Shaking off the sad thought, he gave his sister a demonstrative hug, "We should take the private jet up for a visit sometime." He glared at his brother-in-law as he spoke, justifying the difference between Nebraska and New York with his clear blue eyes.

Tori liked the sound of that and agreed without

hesitation, "Yeah, I guess there will be lots of occasions for us to do things together." Things felt different having actual proof of their relationship. *Somehow, it just seems more real.* Holding her husband's hand as they walked back to the truck, she could see her new life coming together, and hoped the tiny pieces would soon fall into place as well.

What We Can

The two boys arrived at the shop Monday afternoon. Tori and her two men were again working on the latest project when the pair walked up, the oldest looking a bit unhappy to be made to talk to the girl who had become a stranger. Chris had heard some of the stories that were going around, and he no longer felt pleased to be in her company.

Steven seemed less distressed, and babbled away about how his summer had gone, and what his classes were like in the fifth grade. Tori smiled at him, having missed his openness and curiosity. Kneeling down in front of him, she gave him her undivided attention while he explained for several minutes; then she sent him into the house to find a snack.

Turning to the older boy, she put the question directly, "So, is there anything you want to say or ask me? Or do you just wanna assume what you've heard is the truth and be done with it?"

His face twisted in anger, Chris said nothing. Michael wiped his hands with a red shop rag, trying to decide if he needed to stay and help with the conversation, or if he should go in the house to supervise the younger lad.

Brian rose from where he had been squatting and made the call for him. "Let's head inside, give these two a bit of privacy," he suggested. Without argument, Michael followed, leaving them alone for a moment.

"How could you?" Chris demanded in a loud voice.

Startled, Tori tried to remain calm. "How could I what?" she countered in an even tone. "I'm not sure what the stories even are, so you're gonna have to give me a little more to go on."

His hands were clenched tightly into fists, "They say you're a murderer. That you kill people. How could you?"

Tori looked away from him for a moment, collecting her thoughts while she cleaned the work area. "Who says?" she asked quietly, considering what Trish had told her about Michael trying to explain. Somehow, she doubted he would have gone that far.

Briefly, the boy told her what he had heard, and she quickly realized that this was one of the stories her friend had warned her about; something more fun to tell, exciting really, but far from the dark and ugly truth. Shaking her head, she laughed quietly. "Chris, honey, that's a load of bullshit," she tried to be blunt.

"Honestly, no one in this town knows about me, except Michael and Brian. Not where I came from or anything else. The Feds came to get us because of what had happened to my brother in New York, not because of anything I had done." She paused for a moment, peering at him to see what his reaction would be.

Seeing that his face had relaxed, becoming not quite so contorted, she continued, "I had to take care of some things. That's why I didn't come back with them. But I'm home now, and I'm really looking forward to being here for you after school, or whenever." She felt a small jolt of surprise that she actually meant it.

"You're not gonna tell me the real story, are you," he asked her in a quiet, submissive tone.

Shaking her head, Tori did her best to soothe him, "The real story is we do what we can. We do what we have to do. Sometimes those things are hard, and sometimes the choices hurt. But that's how life is."

Walking over to her, the young man raised his arms to hug her. Sliding her arms around his shoulders, Tori lay her cheek across the top of his head. She had no idea when it happened, but somewhere in the past, she had grown to love the sandy-haired boy who never quite trusted people. Rubbing his back a few times, she asked, "You wanna work on the bike today?"

Dabbing his eyes, he sniffled, "Yeah. I really missed coming down here, ya know?" He gave her an awkward grin and the pair went over her checklist of things that the bike required.

Watching him, Tori could tell he had retained a great deal as he seemed to remember many of the things she had taught him during the time they had spent together last spring. Getting their hands dirty, they worked until they were called for dinner. Washing up in the deep sink, she sprayed him with water, causing him to break into laughter and bringing a smile to her own lips.

Inside, the mood remained good-humored around the crowded tiny table. The steaks were delicious, and they even had a bit of ice cream for dessert.

Chris eagerly told Michael and Brian about his classes, being in eighth grade over at the little school that both boys attended. "It's my last year there, since the high school kids all take the bus over to the next town," he lamented.

"Oh yeah? It's a cool way to grow up, though," Brian reassured him, "You'll make some good friends, and maybe even keep them for a lifetime. Me and Chuck became best friends when I moved to Nebraska, and still are." He smiled, but he could feel the conflict taking shape inside of him, knowing time was running out and eventually he would have to go home.

Moving over to the living room after the meal, the guitars were brought out and both boys were allowed to play. Tori had begun instructing them earlier that year, and Brian felt quite impressed with how quickly Steven had been picking up on the process, even with his smaller hands. "Nothing like raw talent," he grinned at the youngster, "And desire. That helps."

While the group carried on, Tori pulled out her notebook, putting more of her music into the proper form. Reading over a few of her older songs, her mind turned, *some of these more recent ones aren't nearly as sad. Hell, someday I may really be able to write happy songs after all.*

Trish knocked on the door at 8:30, and the boys left reluctantly, both faces glowing brightly. Tori felt pleased that Chris still did not know the truth about her ugly history. *Maybe someday he'll be told, when he's older and able to understand the how and why of the way things were, but for now, it's better that he be left in his innocent state, unaware of how cruel the world can be.*

"I think I'll head over to the pub for a bit," Brian announced as soon as they were gone, "See if I can get into a little trouble."

Tori caught sight of his grin and surmised he had begun to miss his old life. *Hanging out in a small town isn't nearly as exciting as the life of a rock star.* As much as she had not wanted him there, the thought of his leaving made her a little forlorn deep inside. "Sure, Danny; have a good time," she forced a small smile to cover her sad thoughts.

As soon as they were alone, Michael stepped up behind his wife. Sliding his hands around her waist, he moved them across her flat stomach and brought them up to cup her swollen breasts. Using his chin, he pushed her hair out of the way and blew into her ear, biting firmly on her lobe.

Tori trembled at the deep wash of emotion the actions produced. *I'm so addicted to this man. Love him so much… I'm so glad I chose him in the end.* Laying her hands over the backs of his, she squeezed, enjoying the tightness the action produced in her chest, "You know this isn't the place for making love."

He had been watching her that day, peeking down her shirt like old times before she took his name. Seeing his mark on her chest had aroused him, and he had been waiting, semi-patiently for the cover of darkness, so that he could be alone with her. Pulling at her clothes, he teased, "Yeah, I was thinking I would fuck you tonight instead."

Tori paused slightly, surprised by his choice of words, "You sure?"

Eagerly, desire driven by the need to please her, "Oh yeah, I'm more than sure," he grinned as he moved to undress her where they were, only locking the door in case Brian were to return too soon.

Tori, being much less shy, did not need any persuading to remove her clothing on the spot. Even the thought of her brother catching them in the act excited her a little. She felt certain he knew about their encounters, as they were a noisy pair, and although they made love every night and most mornings, she couldn't hide her enthusiasm at adding a bit of rougher excitement to their routine.

Languishing on the floor together some time later, their passion spent, they enjoyed the bare bliss of one another's exhausted bodies. Clinging to her from behind, Michael kissed her sweaty skin and tasted her naked flesh, his left hand rubbing her head through her thick mane.

Overcome with deep emotion, he professed, "I love you so much. Please, don't ever leave me again. I really don't think I would survive it." His voice choked slightly at how much he treasured her, surprising her with tenderness after the coarseness of their sex.

Grasping his wandering fingers, she gave him a squeeze and cooed, "You're so good to me. Better than I deserve. And I love you, too."

"You deserve only the best, love; and if you weren't my wife, I would ask you to marry me... all... over... again."

Doctor's Orders

The following morning, Tori noted that Brian had not returned. She had passed on her workout, preparing to make the trip over to the next town for her appointment. *Probably found a local cutie to take to the motel for a romp of his own.* Again, she dolefully considered he would be leaving soon, as he obviously had begun losing interest with hanging around, and the limited entertainment her world had to offer.

With so much on her mind, her palms felt sweaty as she drove, gripping and releasing the wheel nervously. *There's so much pending on what he has to say.* The butterflies joined her as she rolled into the parking lot, and she inhaled deeply to calm them before she went inside.

Entering through the glass door, she checked in with the receptionist, who once again wore the bright red lips and nails, her hair in a long braid this time. Taking a seat in a pink upholstered chair, she did not have long to wait, and the nurse called her back to seat her in the doctor's cubical with the cluttered desk.

A few minutes later, he came in, wearing a toothy grin and announcing, "Well, I have good news. Two fold, really. First off, your tests were both good, as your bone density is within normal limits, and your blood work came back quite favorable. That means we can look for other causes for your sketchy menstruation, but I'm still strongly suspecting the exercise may be closely connected." Having taken a seat, he folded his arms in front of him.

"What I would like to do is called a hysteroscopy, and if I find anything that can be taken care of immediately, it'll be done right then. If we get lucky, we may be able to avoid the larger procedure and cut down on your recovery time as well."

The doctor concluded with a broad smile, and Tori felt ecstatic at the news. "So, what about my exercise? If it's so closely connected, what does that mean, exactly?" she asked him to clarify that point, a smile curling her own lips.

The doctor sat back in his chair, pausing a moment before he gave her the only bad news. "You need to cut back. You're too healthy for your own good. I'm going to recommend you either do one-third less each time than you normally would or you can work out no more than four days a week instead of every day. I'll let you decide how to take care of that."

Her features crumbling, Tori felt sick. She had thought she would be prepared to do whatever it took to have a baby, but the thought of giving up her workouts made her doubt her own resolve.

Seeming to understand her conflicting thoughts, he nodded encouragingly, "I know that can be a difficult thing, and you're not the first person to think so. Working out brings on a euphoric state, essentially a drug. It can be challenging to let go."

Frowning, she knew she would have to take all of this into consideration. "So, exactly what were you looking for, with all of the testing?"

"There's a rare condition that young female athletes can get," the doctor explained, "With three possible effects on their bodies, a triad of sorts. They can get weak bones, which yours are fine. They also may develop eating disorders, which you are not underweight and your blood work came back normal."

"And," he hesitated slightly, "They can get amenorrhea, which is the absence of menstruation. It affects girls and young women, from early teens to late twenties, and they can have one, two, or all three of the conditions. Since your menarche came so late, I strongly suspect the exercise could be a contributing factor. We'll know more when you stop working so hard. And that reminds me, you'll need to start using some type of birth control."

Tori raised her brow.

"In case that's the reason, you could become pregnant once your cycle becomes more normal. If you do have scarring, we don't want that to happen until it's been taken care of." He smiled at her, and her heart began to pound.

Oh my God, I need birth control… so I don't become pregnant. She wasn't sure if the butterflies were there out of excitement, or terror, but they suddenly danced out of control.

Discussing the options, Dr. Lazenby put her on a mild oral contraceptive and told her to back off from the exercise for six months. After that, they would meet to see about doing the procedure and go from there.

Tori felt numb as she paid her bill and made an appointment for six months out as she left. Taking deep breaths, she focused on relaxing as she climbed into her old truck. *Only time will tell baby girl, no use getting tense too soon.*

She found herself in high spirits as she picked up her prescription and drove home, her hopes of having a family brighter than ever before, even if she did have to give up on a bit of her workouts. *Besides, with the Scorpions out of the picture, I don't have to be so worried; so concerned about being at the top of my game any longer.*

Hiding her pills carefully until she had time to discuss them with her husband, Tori carried on business as usual around the house. With only a few days before Brian was to leave, she wanted to spend every moment of that time with him, sharing and doing the things that they loved.

The evening before his departure turned out to be the most difficult for the pair of them to bear. As they finished their dinner and moved into the living room to play together for the last time, the mood was less festive than it had been in weeks.

Noticing his foul features while he held his instrument listlessly and half-heartedly strummed a few riffs, Tori spoke out in anger at his attitude. "I don't see what you're so upset about. You're going home tomorrow, but it's not the end of the world. We'll see each other again, and besides, you miss your life. Admit it."

Brian didn't look up, "I admit it." Tori laughed out loud, the sound surprising him and he lifted his gaze to stare at her. "You have a beautiful laugh," he told her in earnest, "And you don't use it enough."

"I know," her smile lessened a bit at his doleful expression, "But I'm learning."

"It's not too late, ya know." *Fuck me, I promised I would leave her alone*, but he couldn't help himself, "It's spectacular up north when winter comes. You would *love* New Jersey, and I even have that place in Florida. Have you ever lived on the beach?"

Tori only nodded, having heard all of this before, "I know, Danny," she gasped a small sigh as she put her black and white beauty away, "But I don't belong there. I belong here, with Michael and the life we're building."

She thought of her hidden package, smiling to herself. "Please understand, and don't make this any harder than it has to be." Standing, she left him alone, heading to the shower and turning in early to avoid any further badgering.

The next morning, Brian gathered his things, leaving the guitar in the storage with the rest of the band's belongings, in case they ever returned and needed them again.

The mood continued to be bleak as she drove him to San Antonio to his private plane. Overcome by emotion, she clung to him tightly before she allowed him to board it, thanking him for his visit. A tear slipped from her eye as she realized she would miss him.

Driving home alone, Tori wished she had insisted Michael go with her on the long trip. *It would've been crowded on the way down, but this part would've been more pleasant.*

Left alone with her thoughts, she considered her trip to the doctor and the conversation the two of them needed to have. *I know it's not necessary in the immediate future, but it'll have to be soon, and this long, boring ride might have been the perfect time to have it.*

Last Days

Arriving back at their small dwelling in the late afternoon, Tori found Michael in the yard, leaning underneath her favorite tree. He had been making plans of his own, and could wait no longer to take her over to the house and show her what he had been working on.

Hopeful Brian hadn't given away his secret, he grinned at her as she pulled up to park. Climbing out of the vehicle, she greeted him warmly, happy to wrap her arms around him and swing side to side for a long embrace.

In the end, he pulled away from her and grasped her hand, leading her to his bike. "Hop on," he instructed, throwing his leg over and firing it up.

Listening to the purr of the engine, Tori swung on behind him, expecting them to go for a long and relaxing ride. She leaned against him to place her hands around on his chest, happy to live in the moment.

Surprised at the brevity of their trip, they only went a few blocks before pulling into the drive of the large white Victorian that stood a mile from their place. Cutting off the engine, he indicated they had arrived, and she dismounted the motorcycle warily.

Looking around, she noticed how clean and well-kept the place had begun to look. *Wow, someone even painted it,* she observed as they approached the front steps.

As he guided her towards the door, Marge came out to greet them, a full smile on her face. Tori hid her surprise, well aware that the older woman thought of her as trash. Turning to her husband, she could see he suppressed a grin, and she had no doubt that they were up to something.

"Ok, would one of you like to tell me what's going on?" she demanded in a playful tone, her own lips begging to curl at the magic of the mysterious moment.

Allowing his smile to emerge, Michael softly replied, "Marge is going to sell us her house."

Tori stood struck, as if the wind had been knocked out of her. The news daunting, even though it had not been meant to be a bad thing, the girl tried not to show her apprehension. Her eyes darted back and forth between the two of them, not exactly sure how to react. *Surely this is some kind of joke.*

Finally able to smile, she managed, "Well, that's good news, I think. And when did you guys decide this?" She didn't want to appear ungrateful, but having heard the plan, she knew her own plotting could be effected.

Michael shrugged, "I've been coming over to help out since I returned from New York. And we came to the agreement: you and I get to buy the house on one condition... Marge will remain here as long as she lives."

Tori continued to force her smile and play the role at hand, her fingers rubbing gently along the back of her mates as she clung to him. *He planned all this shit without even asking me?* Her thoughts racing, heart pounding, she remained tight-lipped. *I guess two can indeed play at that game.*

Lost in his own excitement and not grasping she was upset, Michael led her inside to show her the work he had already completed, and explain what else they were going to be doing.

Tori followed along in silence, unwilling to unload on him in front of the lady of the house, but inwardly she fumed the entire time he laid out his plans.

Eventually, the tour ended, and she felt like she'd been beaten. *The amount of time the repairs will take, not to mention the expense!* The sun setting as they returned to the veranda she still covered her trepidation. She simply leaned her head on his shoulder, holding him and fighting not to cry.

Still grinning, he had saved his biggest piece of news for last. "And when we finish the house," he whispered quietly, "I want to adopt some kids."

Instantly, Tori's face popped up to stare into his deep brown eyes. *Adopt? I want to have our own!* Her mind spun. Not to slam him in his moment of joy, she clenched her jaw tightly and simply nodded her agreement. *This will need to be discussed, but not here and not now.*

Returning home, they ate a small meal and made their way to bed. She managed to go through the motions, and her mate satisfied himself within her before he drifted off to sleep. Lying naked in the darkness, Tori once again toyed with her wedding band, thinking about living in the oversized house with an adopted brood of children.

It wouldn't be so bad, right? Michael loves me and has worked very hard to arrange all of this for me and for our lives together. Still, she could not help feeling cheated, as if her chance to have a family of her own had been taken from her all over again.

Rising at 5:00 am the next morning, Tori made her run in record time, the turmoil of the past days and weeks still swimming inside her mind. Her off day, the one that she wasn't supposed to exercise, she allowed herself the run, and then passed on the rest of the workout.

Instead, she lay on the ground, staring up at the dark

sky, as it would be another hour before dawn. *I'm going to talk to him about his plans. I can't let this go any further.*

Rising to her feet, she set off on a long and slow walk, hoping to clear her head, and to be calm when they discussed their future. Making it all the way across the tiny town, she found herself in front of the large white structure that her husband so deeply adored.

This house makes me sad... reminding me of the people I left in LA. I truly wish he had consulted me before offering to buy the place. Of course, I wasn't exactly here to be consulted... She felt a stab of guilt twinge her gut as she admitted he was not entirely to blame.

Tori inhaled sharply, seeing the curtain move in an upstairs window. Her heart pounding, she ran her fingers through her hair while she considered running away. *What if I was seen? Oh my God, I can't believe he convinced her to do this.*

Standing still in the lessening darkness, she waited to see what would happen. If she had been spotted, the last thing she wanted to do was run. Pretending as if she were busy making plans, she braced herself to be confronted by the mistress of the property.

Sure enough, just when she thought it had been too long, and it must have not been what she thought, the front door swung wide, and the rounded frame was standing behind the screen. Strangely, the woman smiled at her.

I know the old witch hates me. She's snubbed me enough times; I don't have to be told. The only time the woman had ever spoken to her civilly was in the presence of her husband, a fact Tori did not miss making note of. *I'm quite sure she is selling* him *this house, not me.*

Running her fingers through her long dark hair, she stood gazing down the short street, hoping the other woman would ignore her. It was no use; the old bag began making her way down the step, gripping the rail tightly.

Tori watched her from the corner of her eye, *God she moves so damn slow.*

Smiling as she made her way up to her, Marge greeted her warmly, "Well, ain't this a pleasant surprise! Michael tol' me you'd get over our li'l differences, but I never believed it was true!"

Tori eyed the plump figure suspiciously. "What do you mean by that?" she snapped indignantly.

Marge only nodded, speaking in an exhausted manner, "Le's get inside child. I ain' as young as you, an' it's chilly out here."

She beamed as she spoke, and Tori felt compelled to follow, again thinking that the woman moved too slowly, and considered something seemed out of place with her.

Reaching the steps, Marge stumbled slightly, fumbling before clutching the metal tightly. She took her time to climb, and Tori stood on the ground, staring as her mind slowly took in details of the structure.

Picturing the few times she had been to the house, she realized the porch felt different. *That wasn't here before. Not when George was alive, or when we visited after the funeral.*

Grasping the elder lady's other arm, she guided her up the stairs, "So, you got a new railing." Achieving the perfect tone, Tori prepared to make nice and find out what the hell was going on with the odd pair her husband and the old woman made.

"Yes, yes," Marge's wrinkled lips agreed, "Yur sweet man put that up fur me a few weeks ago, afraid I'd fall down my own porch, I think."

Tori felt thoroughly confused and ashamed at her angry thoughts. Her *sweet man* had led her through the house the evening before, and she hadn't even noticed the new railing. *I was too pissed to pay attention, I guess.* Inside, she peered around more closely, searching for the other things she might have missed.

Sure enough, the railing on the main staircase had also been replaced. *Several of the steps look new as well. Michael is quite the carpenter, after all.*

Moving through the dining room, the pair made their way into the kitchen and Marge spoke in her raspy voice. "I never would'a guessed I'd be sellin' you two my house, neither. That Michael; he's a real smooth talker. The day he came t' ask me, it was th' first thing outta his mouth; '*I want your house,*' he said."

Tori guided her to a chair, kneeling down in front of her to have a closer look. "What's wrong with you?" she asked pointedly, not intending to sound insensitive.

Marge gave her a startled stare, having assumed Michael had filled his wife in on her condition. "He didn' tell you?"

"No," she felt sick, noticing the purple tinge to the older woman's lips, "Do you still have George's oxygen machine?"

"No, no, I don't need that," she reassured, "Jus' need t' sit for a bit. Get too tired if I try t' go too far."

Standing, Tori made her way over to the fridge, searching for a bottle of water. Seeing a large pitcher, she found a glass and poured some for the matriarch, placing it on the table and taking a seat across from her so she could watch her more closely. Marge started to speak again, but Tori hushed her, insisting she wait until she had fully rested.

Anxious and unable to sit still, Tori set about cleaning the kitchen, washing the few dishes that were in the sink and putting them away. About fifteen minutes later, the color had returned to the fleshy lips, and Tori reclaimed her chair, allowing her to explain. "Now, tell me what's going on," she implored.

"I'm dying," the old woman said calmly. "And I'm leaving my house to you!" She sat blinking bright blue eyes for several seconds, allowing the girl to process what she had said. "Michael's been comin' for weeks, checkin' in on me and takin' care o' things here at the house. He tol' me when you got home, you'd come by too, an' you did," her smile emerged, weak, but sincere.

Tori sat stunned, sputtering for a moment as she tried to make a coherent reply. Finally she got the words out, "I don't want your house, Marge."

The older woman looked as if she had been slapped, so Tori clarified, taking in a deep breath and leaning back in dismay, "Michael surprised me with all of this. I know he means well, but I never wanted anything as grand as this." Her eyes shifted around the old kitchen, and she could see the places her husband's hands had touched.

Continuing, she tried to explain, "I'm perfectly happy with the house we have. We have the small bedroom, and I found a doctor willing to help me try to have a baby. Our baby. That's all I want, the chance to try." A tear slipped from her eye, and she caught it as it dripped from her jaw, sniffing loudly.

Marge stared at her in disbelief. "Then what're you doin' here?" she asked in a quiet voice.

"I have no idea, actually," dabbing her eyes with a small chuckle, Tori confessed, "After my run, I just felt the need to come here. As if I were being drawn. Don't get me wrong, it would be a beautiful place… I just don't need this. It's too much for me."

Marge recalled what Michael had told her, about how the girl had been raised. "But you deserve this place," she reassured her, still dazed by the girl's uncertainty. "An' jus' 'cause you live here don' mean you can't try fur a baby o' yur own."

Giving her a smile, she tried to smooth things, "I know, and it's ok. It'll work out. Now, tell me what I can do for you. What do you mean by *dying*?"

The old woman grinned, shaking her head. *Kids. They never understand.*

The two were still sitting, talking in hushed voices, when Michael came up to the front door and let himself in. He gave his wife a small smile and peck on the cheek when he entered the kitchen, pleased his prediction had come true.

"I knew I'd find you here," he teased her gently. Gazing into her soft blue eyes, he noticed the red and wondered if she'd been crying. Kneeling down in front of his bride, he spoke in a quiet tone, "She told you didn't she. I knew you'd take it hard."

Tori didn't bother to argue, and simply pulled him to her so she could hug his head against her chest. *I can't be selfish here, not like this,* and she stifled the urge to cry.

"It's ok," he assured her, "She's got some time. And we're gonna take good care of her." Pulling away, he smiled up at her, patting her on the leg and rising to get started on the chores that needed to be done.

On her feet, Tori relented, "I should run home and change. I'll be back quick as I can to help out," she called over her shoulder as she headed out the front door. She returned in less than an hour and fell easily into her new role.

During the first few days of their new routine, Tori worked hard to reconcile her feelings and not let on how disappointed she had been in their plans for the future. She could not bring herself to crush her husband's dreams or turn her back on the woman who obviously needed them. The couple tried to split their time, he working on the motorcycles in the shop and making repairs on the larger property while Tori took care of Marge.

As she explained it, her old body had simply given out,

which seemed hard for the girl to understand. She had never been around anyone who had been dying of old age, or even very ill, for that matter. She also became deeply upset that the woman hadn't informed her family, and insisted that she do so.

Trish took it especially hard, having lost George only six months before. *At least she'll have some time to prepare*, Tori consoled herself. Distraught over her best friend's impending loss, she threw herself wholeheartedly into the task at hand, for Trish's sake, as well as for her own.

Busy with bathing, dressing and other daily chores, Tori had little time to worry about her own problems. Instead, she pushed them to the back of her mind, refusing to allow her doubts to get the better of her. *I'm strong and I can do this,* she reminded herself firmly. *After all, this is what having family and friends is all about.*

Taking the situation almost as a test of her worth as a human being, the girl began to see a side of life she had never really understood. *I know there have been people who cared for me;* but Tori had never physically cared for someone else.

She only briefly compared it to her time in the company of the Dragons, quickly realizing the difference. *I was their whore, their minion, and this is not the same. This… is worth doing; I need this as much as she does.*

The older woman accepted her help graciously, and the two of them became better friends than the girl would ever have thought possible. The older woman shared tales about her long and ordinary life, and her young nursemaid found herself drinking them in, almost starved for understanding of the things most people take for granted.

I've had so few female friends, and certainly not one with this many years under her belt, she conceded with a heavy heart, keenly aware there was not much time to be had.

After only a few days, Tori approached her husband about the possibility of moving into the house sooner rather than later, and hoped he would accept her reasons for doing so.

"I think Marge would benefit by our being closer. I'm concerned about her safety when we aren't there." She gave him a wide-eyed stare as she made the proposition, a silent plea for him to understand.

Grazing her chin with the back of his fingers, Michael considered how much her behavior surprised him. Nodding, he knew he had no grounds to refuse the request, "Sure, if you think it's time, then we can start the paperwork and I'll take care of moving our things. I know you have your hands full between tending to Marge and the boys."

Throwing her arms around her husband's neck, she shrieked, truly grateful for his trusting nature. *I'm doing this for me,* she confessed to herself, *but no one else needs to know that part.* After all, if she couldn't pass this test, how would she ever expect to care for a family of her own?

Completing the purchase of the property, the couple took a bedroom upstairs. Tori felt her spirits lifted somewhat, aware that her efforts did make a difference to the woman in her care, and she found herself devastated when, only four short weeks later, her charge passed away.

Tori felt strange after the funeral, the family gathered once again at the large old house in the cool fall air. *Things are different*, she noted, *even if they look the same.*

The deed had been transferred at the time they moved in, and the house became officially theirs, but it still felt odd. The community members were kind, and she appreciated their warm sentiments, but in the end, it wasn't enough.

I've lost another friend, she admitted to herself as she grieved in private, and the big empty house became almost more than she could bear. She hadn't told Michael she didn't really want it, as it had been too late to change their minds.

Besides, there were too many reasons to make the best of things, and too few to spoil his joy at giving her the things he felt she needed.

In the end, Tori told herself it should have been happy times, fall setting in full swing and Halloween rapidly approaching. It should have been, but she couldn't shake her feeling that something wasn't right, even after Marge had been laid to rest.

She had spoken to her brother a few times since he left, aware that he had his own demanding life to deal with. When she informed him of the older woman's passing, she had not intended to pressure him to come for a return visit. To her surprise, he eagerly made the trip, seizing the opportunity to spend time with his younger sibling in her time of sorrow.

He flew in the week after the funeral, but even having him close did not ease her mind. That old familiar feeling of waiting for the other shoe to drop had her in its grasp, and she could almost feel the darkness lurking. *It's out there, waiting to overtake us*, and nothing she did seemed enough to push the awareness away.

Life of a Star

Things had been strangely tense around the small family during Brian's second visit. *Well, he seems pretty pleased to be back to his old life,* Tori assessed as she whisked around the kitchen making dinner; *the life of a star.* She felt happy for him. *He loves his life, and I love mine,* she told herself for the umpteenth time since his arrival.

The back door opened and Michael noisily joined them, "How's dinner coming?"

"Almost ready," she smiled at her mate. "Wash up and have a seat, love."

Obedient to the letter, he washed his hands and dried them on a small towel, then laid the plaid piece of cloth across the edge of the sink. Observing his wife's stiff movements, he wondered if the pair had had a fight. Catching her, he looped an arm around her waist and looked her in the eye, "You ok?"

He used German, which startled her, "I'm fine," she shot back in kind, a stab of guilt at their rudeness. Pulling away, she went on with preparing the meal.

Taking the chair across from their company, "How're things with you?" His voice sounded non-committal, polite as always.

"I'm good. Glad to be home. The guys were pretty

relieved that I made it back, too. Afraid I might decide to stay here and give up on them altogether, I guess." He laughed, a bit anxious about his choice.

"That's good," Michael agreed, "At least you know they missed you. You're headed back tomorrow, right? Whirlwind visit?"

Brian had arrived the previous afternoon and would be leaving the next day, but he ignored the jab. "Yeah, maybe they did. More likely upset they would have to replace me. That'd be a pain in the ass. The group wrote some great music during our time here in Texas, though. We're pretty eager to get back into the studio and put it into an album, so that'll be our next step." Watching her as she flitted around, he couldn't really tell if she were even listening to him.

"They're making sure to allow me time to see you along the way, too. Even with the busy schedule that a new album will mean." This time, she smiled at him, and he breathed a small sigh of relief. "And I'll be calling you, at least once a week."

Michael grinned, "See, love? That old phone may come in handy after all!"

Tori didn't bite, only shaking her head in response. *I'm tired of debating with him over my brother, and how he thinks he's always right.*

"Our place is back to normal, too. You can't even tell anything happened there." He spoke of the estate in New Jersey, of course, his voice picking up a hint of excitement.

"That's good, hun. I'm really glad those guys didn't tear up all your stuff from mom and dad, either," Tori agreed, placing food on the table.

"Yeah, that would've been a real tragedy." He paused, at the part that mattered the most, and would most likely get a reaction, "And we set up one of the bedroom suites for the two of you. You know, in case you ever wanna come visit."

He watched her keenly, not sure how she would take his gentle prodding.

Tori laughed quietly, actually expecting it, "That's really sweet, hun. I bet it's real nice." *And I bet I don't ever see it. But, he's only here for a short time, no need of letting this upset me.* "Maybe we could go for a few days, say at Christmas?" She gave Michael a wide-eyed gaze for effect, hoping this time it would work.

Michael glanced over at his brother-in-law, shaking his head. He then shot his wife a surprised look, "We can't do that! It'll be our first Christmas as husband and wife! I thought we would spend it here... in our new home..." he eyed her coyly, tugging at her heartstrings with his tender stare.

With a shrug and a chuckle, she let the subject drop. *He has some excuse every time it's mentioned. And of course Brian is leaving tomorrow, but at least he came.* Things had changed between the two men, she felt sure of it. *Part of the darkness, I guess; with me caught in between.*

Her brother grinned slightly, "Well, if you won't come to me, maybe I can make it back here." He felt uneasy making the suggestion, unsure if they would want him if it were going to be that special. "We're doin' another promo in LA here in a few weeks, but I should be free to make the trip by then. Or Thanksgiving. Whenever you'll have me. You know." He shrugged, feeling like an outsider begging to be let in.

"LA, wow. Seems so long ago." Tori's mind became instantly swept away, a stab of jealousy at his ability to return there, *or go anywhere he wants, for that matter*, so easily. Pushing the sad thoughts away, "Sure, Christmas will be fine," she turned to smile at him, "I'll plan on seeing you then. A longer visit, under better circumstances."

"Yeah, come anytime, bro," Michael's grin spread

wide, maybe too wide.

Brian pursed his lips before he accepted the offer. He could tell something had been bothering her, but wasn't about to ask what. "Ok, Christmas it is," he smiled as well.

Tori felt relieved the arrangements had been settled, and the three of them could eat their meal in peace. *I wish they wouldn't do this to me,* her thoughts scattered as they ate. The conversation had shifted, but she could still feel the tension, as if they were pulling at her, each wanting her to take their side in some hidden battle between them. *When did this happen?* she wondered as she slowly chewed. *Or has it always been here, and I just never knew?*

Brian had rented a car for the trip, and they bid farewell at the shop after brunch at the diner. Standing next to the vehicle, bag at his feet, he found himself making small talk, "You know, we need to put in a private airport around here. Or see about finding one I can fly into that's a bit closer."

"Yeah, would be nice," Tori grinned, then squinting at him, she took the plunge, "I love you." Her words sent a flutter of surprise across his features.

"I... love you too! Wow, I hadn't realized you had made it that far!" He grinned ear to ear as he reached to hug her.

"Yeah, me either," she slapped him on the back as she clung to him, "But I missed you last time after you left, so I thought I better say it for real. Be careful out there, ok?" Tori hadn't wanted to spook anyone with her creepy intuitions, but with him leaving again, she suddenly felt the need to have her feelings known.

"Sure thing, sis." He cast a wayward look around the shop, "I guess you really love doing this, don't you."

Tori's lips curled, "Yeah, I guess you could say that. It'll be a nice living for us, too." *Now what's he up to? Or is he just stalling...*

Pursing his lips, Brian continued warily, "I've been thinking about that. You shouldn't have to make a living at something you love."

Taking a shocked step away from him, "Why not?" she demanded, then snapped with a frown, "You do."

Eyes darting to meet hers, he had walked into that one and knew he needed to change tactics. "Fair enough. What I meant was, you should have another way to make money." Her brow furrowed deeper.

"What exactly is this about, Danny?" her arms crossed in anger, "You're leaving and can't go without insulting me first?" *Or was that another jab at Michael?* The two of them had been sparring with words since his arrival and she was about sick of it.

"Uh, no," his shoulders slumped in defeat. Sighing deeply, he leaned over and withdrew a folded set of pages from the side of his bag. Handing them to her, he accepted his choice, "This is for you."

Unfolding the papers, Tori found a check in the center of the sheaf, made out to her in the amount of $12,486. Staring at it, she could feel the rage seething inside her, "And what the fuck is this for? I don't want your money!"

"It's not mine," he countered evenly, "It's yours. It's part of your share of mom and dad's estate." She stared at him coldly as he reached over to show her the pages behind the check. "See? I had it put into a fund for you. Your half of our inheritance, plus interest from the twenty years it sat, untouched. Plus, I bought out your half of the farm, with interest there as well."

Her jaw dropped as she stared at the sum, just shy of a million dollars. "I... I can't take this," she stammered, shoving the sheets towards him.

"You don't have a choice. It's done. The check is three months-worth of income from the fund, so you'll only get about a third of that each month, but it should be more than enough to live in this dinky little town." He paused, smiling, "And you control the rest. The broker's contact information is there, so you can get in touch with them if you want to change how any of it's invested."

Jaw open wide in disbelief, "I don't know what to say," she whispered airily, still staring at the pages.

"Thank you, that's what you say." His straight white teeth gleamed, "And you're very welcome." Reaching for her again, arm encircling her tightly, he breathed into the dark hair that matched his own, "I love you, Nikki. And I'm so glad that you were found. Don't ever think that I'm not."

Not expecting a reply, he stooped to gather his bag. A peck on her cheek, he climbed into the car and off he drove, leaving her to push aside her dark feelings, and hope for the best, a cloud of dust hanging in the air behind him.

Settled

That night, Tori realized she had begun to feel a little better about being in their new home. Her off days of exercise were becoming tolerable, and she had settled into a routine, now that Marge no longer needed full-time care. *Maybe things are going to work out after all,* she told herself as she got ready for bed.

The couple made love that night and the following morning as usual before Michael went down to make breakfast for them. Dragging her feet after her shower, she took her pill in private. *I guess I need to set aside time to talk to him since things are calming down. Not sure what I'm going to say exactly though; I've kept it a secret for so long... I don't want him to think I was hiding it from him.* But deep down she knew in a way she had been, still terrified of where it might lead.

She had hit the second section of sugar pills in her pack the day before, still considering them as she made her way down the stairs. *I wonder if it'll take the entire six months for them to work.* Pushing the subject out of her mind, she joined in the making of the meal with a small sigh.

Fortunately for her, they planned to work on the house that day. She felt odd shortly after breakfast and made a second trip to the bathroom to discover she had started her first actual period in six years. The sight of it scared her a bit. *Oh my God, this is real! Michael is going to be so surprised! And thank God I stocked up on supplies,* she smiled at her own forethought as she pulled the boxes out from under the sink, briefly thinking of LA.

Cleaning up her mess, she understood she would have to take the pills faithfully. *We don't want to conceive before we're ready. Especially before I've had a chance to warn him it could happen*, she thought with an excited grin. *And the doctor wants to be sure I'll be able to carry the baby once it's inside me.* Feeling immense joy, she toyed with the idea of sharing her secret.

Gazing around the place, she could almost feel the house growing on her as her enthusiasm swelled. Freeing her vivid imagination, she allowed herself to consider the experiences their child would have growing up in the stately old structure. *Maybe this wasn't such a bad idea after all.* She contemplated the possibilities as she bounced down the freshly painted staircase, fingers trailing the banister.

Returning to her work on the kitchen cabinets with new diligence, she thought about how soon they could have the major repairs completed. *I bet we could have the house in order by Christmas. And then I could begin adding all the small details and decorations that will make the house a home!* She had already begun imagining new curtains and color schemes.

By the time they made their way to bed that night, Tori had even chosen the room that would be the nursery, adding fuel to her newfound joy in their larger setting. Laying her husband down, she set about taking care of him with her talented mouth and tongue, eager to please him before they drifted off to sleep at the end of a perfect day.

The next morning, Tori trotted over to the diner for her off day. She had come to find that having an alternate and equally pleasing activity planned helped make her new routine easier to stick with, and visiting with her best friend was such an occasion.

The clink of the bell on the glass door a happy, familiar sound, she smiled as she took her seat at the counter and observed Trish, who poured coffee for more of the locals. Glancing through the portal to the back, she noticed an unfamiliar face moving around in the kitchen, *hmmp, I thought I had met everyone in town.*

"Good morning, sunshine," Trish presented her usual glass of ice water with a festive flare, "Coffee today?"

"No, thanks," Tori half smiled, tossing her chin towards the back, "Who's the new guy?" She noticed the sparkle in the older woman's eye as she beamed.

"That," she grinned uncontrollably, leaning on the counter to get closer, "Is Larry. Fresh out o' the navy he is. Retired."

Tori heard herself laugh, "Wow, you seem pretty excited about another cook!" Keeping her voice low, she teased her friend eagerly, "Is he single?"

A pretty pink flush rising up her neck, "Yeah, but it don' matter. He's only here fur a short bit. Stayin' with his brother. You know, Phil Porter, out on his ranch. Only workin' here until he gets settled in a bigger town." The dreamy expression on her face looked refreshing as she glided away to pour more caffeine for her patrons.

Tori was still lost in thought when her husband slid onto the seat next to her, "Mornin' love," he cooed with a silly drawl, happy to see her perkiness had returned since the funeral.

"Hey," she smiled back, then indicated the man still moving around behind the wall. "I think it's time we rented out our old place."

"What?" he demanded in a shocked tone, "I thought

you said it meant too much to you. You didn't want to have someone else living in it." He had been after her for weeks to rent the apartment, and it surprised him that she would suddenly be ready to concede.

Tori shrugged, "Yeah, I did." She paused and chewed her lip, knowing she had only refused before because he pushed her to do it, and she didn't like to be pushed. Sentiment had been an excuse, easily disposed of, "But, he's a middle-aged man, a quiet bachelor, which means our property would be in good hands. Besides, he makes Trish giggle."

Michael laughed out loud, "Oh, he does, does he?" He swung his gaze around to observe the rounded figure still bouncing about the room. "Ok, I'll find out if he's interested," a bit in awe that his bride would play match maker.

"Thank you, love," she kissed her mate, and they enjoyed their breakfast together before making their way down to the shop to begin their day.

Twist of Fate

Tori's fingers trembled as she fitted the bolt through the opening, *damn it, dropped the nut.* Her hand patting the concrete beneath her, she drew a few deep breaths. *Relax, baby girl. You can do this.*

Kneeling next to a motorcycle, she worked to finish her latest build. *At least that's what it looks like I'm doing,* she confessed inwardly. In reality, she waited for her husband to arrive at the shop. *I have to talk to him. Now. I can't put it off any longer.*

Tori had menstruated for the second time in as many months, and she knew to delay any longer would be absurd. *What am I so afraid of? That he'll be upset? That he'll say no?* She had already gone over this conversation with herself before, but apparently she needed to have it again.

Halloween had just passed, and the air cooler as fall settled over the small Texas town. She had made her way to the shop alone that morning; her husband had wanted to finish the final winter preparations on the house, in case they had a cold snap before Thanksgiving.

So, she informed herself firmly, *when he gets here, this is what you're gonna do. First off, you're gonna breathe. Second, you're gonna look him in the eye... and not cry.* Gulping more air, she pushed it out through her dropped jaw noisily. *Fuck me, this is harder than I thought it would be. I just need to spit it out. To hell with the plan. He loves me, he'll understand.*

A few blocks away, back at their house, Michael had finished with the furnace and dropped his tools into the large box. *I wonder if she's ready for an early lunch?* He contemplated the day's agenda with a small smile and checked the time, *damn. Only nine. Too early for lunch.*

He surveyed the current condition of their home as he reached the front door. *Things are really coming along for us;* he ran fingers through his brown curls with a smile of satisfaction. Hearing the jingle of the phone, his heart gave a startled jolt. *Still not used to that damned thing. Maybe we should go ahead and take it out, like she wants.*

He had convinced her to keep the line in case of emergencies, but hardly anyone who knew them had the number. *Brian calls, that's about it.* Another jingle plinked out of the hallway. *Terry and the Tates have it, I made sure of that.* Another ring. *More than likely, it's for Marge.* Yet another ring. *Or another salesman.* He waited at the door for the sound to stop; it didn't. *Well fuck, that's twelve.*

Deciding he better take the call, he made his way over and lifted the receiver to Marge's authentic rotary style phone, calmly stating, "Hello," into it.

On the other end, the voice of Terral Huffman came in an excited eruption, "Mike? Where's Tori? I need to talk to her, it's urgent!"

Surprised, Michael spoke in an even tone, "Hey, Terry; calm down, sir. Tori's down at the shop, but I can let her know you called."

"Naw, man; you gotta get her, right now!" Terry demanded hurriedly, "We got an emergency here. There was a big pile up out on the highway, and *Indelible's* car was involved."

Michael felt the air sucked from his chest, "Holy shit!"

"Yeah, no kidding. Go get her. I'll get some plane tickets set up for you guys to claim in San Antonio. You have a cell number I can reach you at?" His irritation at the couple's shunning of technology became glaringly obvious.

"No, but we'll pick up a go-phone or something and call you from it as soon as we're able. Are you sure it's that serious? I mean, they were actually hurt? I hate to scare the hell out of her and drag her out there…"

"Look. I'm not family and they won't tell me anything. I even tried to pull strings and couldn't get anything concrete. But I do know for a fact that all four of the guys were taken to the hospital by ambulance." He paused, unsure how to break the rest, "And I heard that one of them didn't make it."

"Oh my God," Michael's hand shook as he gripped the ancient device. *No way. No way life could be that cruel to her. Not when she's…* "Get the tickets. We'll be in touch as quick as we can. Give us three hours at least to get there, four if you're able."

Terry agreed to the task, and they hung up the phone. Michael knew he needed to get Tori to LA without delay. Feeling as if he'd been stomped, he dashed upstairs and threw two changes of clothes into their packs for each of them.

Locking the front door as he left, he hopped on his bike and pulled up at the shop in short order. Walking up behind his beloved, Tori heard his heavy steps, still preparing herself to share her news. She stood to face him as she had done on the day she had married him, but seeing his face today startled her, as he looked far more than haggard.

"What's wrong?" she queried as he grabbed her arms and leaned his forehead against hers. She could hear his ragged breathing and it gave her chills of fear, knowing he wasn't the kind of person to panic without a reason. *And I haven't even said anything yet!*

Raising a hand to caress the side of her face, he steadied his voice and replied, "There's been an accident."

Searching his eyes as he pulled away from her slightly, there were too many people she cared about to even begin to guess who he meant. An instant later, she didn't have to guess. She knew it was Brian. "In LA?" she asked in a timid voice, to which he simply nodded.

"I packed our bags, and Terry is setting up a flight for us. We need to lock up and move out right now."

She quickly agreed, then faltered, "But I need to run home. I have to be sure I have everything I'll need." *He wouldn't have known to pack my pills*, she realized anxiously. *He doesn't know that I'm taking them.*

Giving her a questioning glare, he reluctantly agreed, "All right, go, and I'll lock up here."

Driving over to her home in the old brown truck, Tori hurried inside while clutching her freshly packed bag. Finding the package where she had hidden it, she stuffed it eagerly inside. Even under the stress of the situation, she felt a small smile on her lips as she thought about the success they had already had with the return of her periods.

Relocking the house, she made her way back to her truck to find Michael already in the driver's seat, waiting for her. His face drawn by deep lines, she could see his flat calm. Taking the passenger side, Tori dropped her bag beside his, on the seat between them.

"We need to let Trish know we're leaving," he pointed out as they pulled into the diner. "She'll need to make arrangements for the boys until further notice." Making the stop short and sweet, they were immediately back on the road, each with news to share during the long drive.

Tearing down the narrow highway as fast as he dared,

Michael dove in first, "Terry didn't have any real information. There was a pile-up of cars, and all four band members were transported. They know that one of them didn't make it, but they haven't announced who." His voice dropped as he gave her a sideways glance, "Presumably they want to notify next of kin."

Tori felt sick, her heart pounding out of control. "Next of kin. They can't notify them until they arrive. They're waiting for me to get there."

"We don't know that!" he snapped. Hands patting the steering wheel, he spoke more calmly, "Let's not jump to conclusions. It could be they haven't reached..." his voice trailed away. "Besides, I think they would have done it by phone if it were you."

Tori stared at his profile, clenching her jaw in thought. "Maybe so. And if he's hurt, he'll need me."

"Yeah," her mate picked up on the thread of hope. "He needs you. That's why we're going."

They rode for nearly an hour in mutual quiet, each turning thoughts about the mysterious phone call and what lay ahead. Tori stared out the window as the grass covered terrain zoomed by. *I should tell him. This is my chance.* But somehow sharing the news felt wrong, dirty in light of what had happened, and what loomed before them.

"You know, you've been acting pretty strange lately. Ever since your brother left the first time. I thought it was the whole thing with Marge, but maybe not. Anything you're ready to talk about?" Breaking the silence, he really wanted to ask about the special trip back to the house, but couldn't bring himself to be that specific; that demanding.

Tori only blinked as she peered through the glass, "I have a lot on my mind." She gripped her hands firmly, petrified.

"Uhuh. Well, we got at least another hour of road

ahead of us. Maybe it would help to talk it out." Tori heaved a deep sigh, swinging her gaze to look at him.

"You know me too well, you know that?" she half smiled. *He really does love me.*

Nodding in an exaggerated fashion, he agreed, "Yeah, we're quite a pair." He turned quickly flickering a grin, "And you're safe with me in every way, remember?"

Tori smiled, feeling her spirits lifted by his strength. *Well, I have an opening.* Unzipping her bag, she calmly produced the pack of small colored tablets and held it so that he could see it.

Shifting his eyes over and grasping what the shiny plastic contained, he struggled to keep the vehicle in line, "Are those... What I think they are?" He wanted to look her in the eye as she explained herself to him, almost enough to stop the truck on the side of the road, but he knew they didn't have time for that.

Shifting their bags into the passenger floorboard, she slid over into the middle seat next to him and buckled the lap belt to look straight ahead. Breathing deeply, she clarified in a shaky voice, "I went to see a doctor. Before Brian left. He examined me, ran some tests, and gave me the pills." She paused, still conflicted by her feelings of excitement during their current set of circumstances. "I go back to see him next year, and we'll know more then."

Michael gripped the wheel tensely as she spoke. He wished she had mentioned all of that sooner, but realized it must have been difficult for her to reconcile with her past. His right hand releasing its grasp, he laid his arm behind her shoulders and pulled her against him, grazing the top of her head with a quick kiss.

They rode the rest of the way in silence, each of them lost in their own thoughts. Stopping at a chain store, they purchased a go-phone, and Tori activated it nervously.

Pulling into the long term parking, they grabbed their bags and pushed through the terminal. A quick call from the device and they had the information to pick up their tickets. There weren't any new details to be had, so Michael hung up the phone and they made their way to catch their plane, which departed a short time later.

Being her third time in the air, Tori wasn't so nervous about the flight, but she felt far from relaxed as the aircraft taxied out and lifted off the runway. Michael held her hand, stroking it lovingly to reassure her. Leaning over, he decided to distract her with a quiet conversation, and began with, "So, you think you'll really be able to have a baby?"

His question startled her in her anxious state, but a smile teased her lips. "The doctor gave me the birth control to prevent it from happening before he's able to treat my scarring, and I've already had two real periods since being on them, right on schedule."

Michael nodded, "Yeah, I noticed them, but I didn't realize it was such a big deal. I mean, girls do that sort of thing." He found himself smiling at this small glimmer of hope despite the dark times around them.

"You're not upset?" she asked in a meek voice.

"Upset? Hell no, I'm not upset! My God, love, can you imagine? And here I go suggesting we should adopt a few, all the while you were sitting on this bit of news. I don't think I could have kept that secret!" He laughed at her, understanding her well-practiced talents in deception.

"It wasn't that easy," she admitted as she shook her head. "If it hadn't been for your surprise, and then all that needed to be done after that, I would've let you in on it weeks ago." He looked a bit hurt, so she continued, "I'm not unhappy about it. Marge needed us, and I'm glad we were able to be there for her. It only meant some things had to wait."

Leaning over, he kissed his wife, "Yeah, we do make a good team, you and I."

Tori grinned, and he allowed her to gush about her feelings and plans now that she could freely do so. Before they knew it, the *fasten seatbelt* light lit up, and they were landing at LAX. Exiting the tunnel, Terry greeted them briefly, and they walked quickly, able to bypass the baggage claim and head straight out to his awaiting vehicle.

Tori took the back seat, content to allow the two men to share the front. Looking anxiously out the windshield and then side windows, she asked, "Is there any more news?" Gravely, Terry shook his head, and she could see that he was distraught, so they rode mutely the rest of the way.

They arrived at the hospital forty-five minutes later and made their way inside. The waiting room appeared packed with people, as there were many others brought in from the pile up, and other families were there as well.

Searching for the studio executive that they had expected to meet them, they finally located him standing against a wall, drinking from a Styrofoam cup. The group made their way over to announce their arrival and catch up on whatever there was to be heard. Reaching to grasp her husband's hand, Tori braced herself, knowing the odds were with her, but in a situation like that, even those odds weren't good.

Faith

Terry studied the tall, dark haired woman, trying to appear nonchalant about it. *She's as beautiful as ever,* he noted her dark curls shimmering in the florescent glare of the hospital lighting. Sighing deeply, he wished he knew more about her present life, but she had not contacted him since abruptly leaving LA the previous year.

He had spoken to her husband a few times, when Brian had been targeted and identified, as well as when they moved into their current home. *A good man to keep us updated that way.* He had also learned a few details from her brother in the last few days, prior to the accident. Other than that, what had become of her was a mystery to him.

She glanced over at him, catching him staring at her, and smiled. Surprising him, she stepped over and slid her arms around his neck in a tight embrace, and he raised his own to pull her against him snugly in return.

I wondered if Mike'll be upset about me hugging on his wife, but shooting him a quick glance, he saw that the other man grinned. Relieved, he relaxed as his hands moved up her spine in a caring motion.

Pulling away slightly, Tori picked up their Russian, like old times, "I met your friend. I've been visiting with him on occasion since I moved away."

Terry only stared at her for a moment, not sure what she meant. Then, he remembered their trip to his small white church the day he shared his faith. The news made him smile, "Oh yeah? That's good to hear."

That'll help her find peace in her life, peace that she deserves. Nodding, he released her, not wanting to cling to her too long. Michael reached over to guide her closer to him, circling her lightly in a possessive loop about her waist.

They knew they might have a long wait, and it disconcerted them that they had not been told for sure which band member had been killed. *However, I'm more or less certain it wasn't Brian,* Tori consoled herself. *If it had been, I would've been informed as soon as I arrived.* Continuing to shift her weight anxiously and leaning slightly against her mate, she felt relieved that he was at least alive.

Eventually, Mark Holt, the band's manager, came out. Reaching out to Michael, he shook his hand vigorously, "Good to see you, Mike." Giving the girl a nod, he waited for the introduction, although he had already been informed that she was Brian's sister.

Wow, sniveling little guy this is. Is that outfit a throwback from the 70's? Tori looked him up and down, disgusted with the puny little man who tried too hard to look like a bad boy, gold chains and all. She felt a surge of guilt at her belittling thoughts, not normally the one to judge people so harshly, and blaming the stress of the occasion.

"Glad to meet you," he shook her hand as well. "Your brother has been stabilized and you'll be able to see him shortly."

Upon hearing the news, Tori forgot everything else and burst into tears, the first she had allowed herself to cry. Gripping her tightly, Michael tried to calm her, he himself relieved that his brother-in-law still breathed, for her sake.

"How're the rest of the guys doing?" he asked in a

hushed tone.

Mark heaved a large sigh. "Collin and Cody are also doing better, and it was Chuck who had been killed. Died on impact." Seeing Tori grip her husband more tightly, he pushed aside the urge to elaborate on the guys, opting for the big picture.

"Twenty-two cars and trucks had been involved by the end. I'm really glad you two were able to make it out here so quickly, you know… just in case." Something in his final words gave Michael a chill, but he refused to inquire further.

A short time later, they made their way to the cafeteria for a meal, where they grazed in an edgy thought-filled quiet. When they were finished, they were taken upstairs, where a smaller waiting room, less crowded, afforded them cushioned seats to rest on.

Late evening had arrived, and Tori grew anxious to see her brother. Only having to wait a bit longer, Mark finally came and escorted the couple to the room where their family member lay awake and waiting for them.

Walking down the hall, the sights and sounds reminded Tori of her own hospital experience, and she clasped Michael's hand bravely as they entered the wide door to his room.

Brian relaxed in a half elevated position, not fully sitting, but not lying flat, either. Seeing her, he gave a weak smile and she began to cry all over again.

Darting over to the side of the bed, she reached with trembling fingers to touch him. His face had been cut in small places in an odd checkered pattern, probably by flying glass, and bruises easily seen on his flesh and around both eyes. "Hi," he breathed and raised his hand to catch hers, lacing their fingers.

Using a hushed voice, "How're you feeling?" she inquired.

He gave a small chuckle, "Like shit." His bluntness caused a tiny laugh to escape her, and the tension level dropped slightly after their brief levity.

"He has a concussion," Mark spoke up, "But other than that, he escaped with rather minor injuries. They had been waiting for him to regain consciousness before drawing any conclusions about his condition, and I think we're in the clear."

Brian, managing a larger grin, "Thanks for being here, Mark. I'll see you later," effectively dismissing the outsider so they could be alone.

Grasping at his hand, she smiled through her tears, "You know; I'm not leaving this room until you do."

"Yeah, I get it. Stubborn as ever." His lips still curled slightly, not the least bit upset about it. He swallowed hard, and she could see his Adam's apple move in his neck. "You know about Chuck, huh?"

A tear ran down her cheek as she stared into the crystal blue eyes that matched hers, "Yeah, they told us. I'm so sorry, Danny. I know he meant a great deal to you."

He squeezed her hand at the use of his old name, loving the way she obviously cared for him. *She came to me. If I had known it would be that easy, I'd have had an accident on purpose.*

It had grown very late by that time, and Michael quietly interjected, "Hey love, I think it's time we let him get some rest."

"That's fine," she quickly replied, "But I'm not leaving this room. I'll sleep on the floor in the corner if I have to."

Her husband relented with a tired grimace, "Nahah, no corners, love. Take the couch instead."

Brian reached over, punching the red button on his emergency nurse control, and waited. When the reply came over the speaker, he called out in gravely exhaustion, "Yeah, we need a couple o' extra blankets in here, and a pillow if you can swing it. Thanks babe!" He gave his sister a wink, and a few minutes later the items were produced.

Taking her place on the cushions and breathing deeply, Tori waited for sleep to find her. She thought about how close she had come to losing the only family she had, *blood family, anyways.* Listening to the beep and hum of the machines in the darkness, she knew she would not be going back to Texas anytime soon, *whether Michael likes it or not.*

Holding On

Brian eagerly ate breakfast the next morning while they watched, talking quietly around him. The doctor would be in shortly and he would more than likely be released; good news, as Tori had no fondness for such places, and had been ill at ease since their arrival.

"Cody and Collin are also doing well," Mark gave them an update. "They should be going home today or tomorrow, too."

Tori only half listened, lost in thought. *It's strange how the four friends were in the same car, in the same accident, but one of them paid a much higher price than the rest, having taken the brunt of the force.* She washed his face, taking over in a mothering manner, which he allowed with a sheepish grin.

"Anyways, just checking in. I'll be back shortly," the group's manager made for the exit, not wanting to overstay his welcome.

Shortly after, a nurse came in to give Brian a few directions. "Go ahead and move around, have a shower, and the doctor'll be by to evaluate you afterwards."

Tori noticed the way her brother leered at the cute little blonde. *He must be feeling at least somewhat better.*

After her departure, he climbed stiffly out of the bed.

"Wow, this's tougher than I thought it'd be." He groaned uncontrollably when he put weight on his legs.

"Easy, baby…" Tori reached to help him stand, "Take your time."

Leaning against her, he pushed himself upright to get his balance. Moving towards the small bathroom, she allowed him to do that part on his own. Waiting, she and Michael sat on the couch and talked about possible scenarios.

"Maybe we could convince him to go home with us," Michael spoke softly.

Tori nodded her agreement, but she doubted that would happen. "If he won't, you know I'm going to stay with him for a while. At least I plan to if he'll let me," her voice low with concern.

Grasping to smooth a stray hair for her, he nodded, "You know he wanted to take you home with him, so I'm sure you won't get any arguments from him." He had surmised she would be holding on to her brother a lot tighter, at least for a while, and had no plans of making her feel badly about it.

Relief crossed her face when Brian exited the tiny room, a wave of steam following him out. He moved gingerly, but all his limbs seemed to be working, and he looked much better with his hair clean and all the blood washed away from his visible skin. Sliding back into his bed, she could tell he was sore, and probably would be for several days. He had donned a pair of jeans, and his bare chest displayed a few cuts and bruises as well.

While waiting for the doctor, Mark and Terry joined the group, ready to help make arrangements for getting him out of the hospital without being mobbed.

Brian nodded when informed that a large group of people had begun to gather out front of the building, "Yeah, that's no surprise."

It became obvious Michael wanted to handle the situation when he tossed out, "So, who's going to set up the escape route?"

The other men were quick to defer to his judgment. Exiting the room, he went to scout the path he wanted to take, leaving them to plan what would happen after they made it out of the room and into the car.

Tori timidly made her suggestion, "I have a huge house in Texas. Out of the way, and perfect for a long recuperation."

Brian refused flat out, "Oh no, I have seen all of the Lone Star State that I care to for a while. I have a house in Florida, and that's where I wanna go." He knew he could rest in privacy there, and they could make their plans for the future more solidly when he had healed.

She could tell he was taking the loss of his band mate rather hard, and knew the two of them were the closest of the four. *They had met when Brian moved in with our grandparents, and had been best friends ever since,* she recalled what he had shared. The other two members were his friends, but for not nearly as long, having formed the group for the purpose of making music, first and foremost, in high school.

The doctor made his appearance while Michael was out, having the young man stand and go through a few evaluation procedures. "I think you're good to go," he finally conceded.

"Will he be safe for flight?" Tori inquired.

"Sure, he can fly. Just make sure the destination is somewhere he can rest. Give yourself a few weeks to recoup and check in with another physician when you get there." He smiled, bringing much-needed relief into the cramped space.

Mark left the small gathering to arrange for their private plane to be ready at the airport. Tori moved about, tossing what little he had there in the room into a plastic bag so they could depart once Michael had decided what the plan would be.

The band's manager had brought in a plain blue tee for Brian to wear, and she liked how it brought out the blue in her sibling's eyes, smiling slightly to reassure him. Noticing his difficulty in getting his stiff body to bend over, she helped her brother with his socks and shoes, overjoyed with the prospect of being able to take care of him. *Amazing how often I end up playing nurse to people,* she recalled, not the least bit upset about it at the moment.

Again, Mark stopped in to provide updates, "Ok, Cody and Collin are also being released. Since Brian is headed to his place, they've decided to take a rest themselves, so they're going to Nebraska. Each will be home with family and friends for a couple of weeks, and I then hope you guys can get together in New Jersey so we can decide what we should do with the band."

Brian nodded, "Yeah, we're pretty broken right now. But it'll keep until we're healed, or at least on the way to healed before we decide anything."

Michael returned to the room while they were hashing things out, having secured a path down a staff elevator on the back side of the hospital and had a car waiting for Brian, Tori and himself.

"We ready?" he inquired sharply, in full bodyguard mode.

"Yeah," Brian agreed as he bid his manager and friend farewell.

Terry chimed in, "I'll help you guys get downstairs, in case you have any problems."

"Appreciate it, man." Michael grinned broadly, pleased with Tori's friend.

Wheeling him out, things went smoothly. Tori

watched around them as they moved, feeling deeply protective of her only brother. Inside the elevator, she stood beside his chair and stroked his dark hair that matched her own, remembering how they had bristled at one another the last time they were in LA together. *Odd how neither of us had noticed how much we look alike at the time.*

On the ground floor, the group made it out through the emergency entrance and climbed into a simple late model sedan. *Smart thinking,* Tori subconsciously praised her spouse. *Few would be expecting to see him in an ordinary car with his flashy lifestyle.* Making straight for the airport, they were met at the front by a group of security, who brought a second wheelchair in case he needed it.

Upon seeing it, Brian tossed out casually, "Naw, I got this."

Giving him a dubious glare, Michael insisted, "Ok, walk. We can bring it along, just in case."

Three hundred yards later, Brian stopped the procession to take a seat in the empty device. Tori's face grew strained as she gazed down at him, *I wonder if he's really ok*; she knew all about the fronts some people put up to hide the truth from those around them.

Making it to the plane's loading area, the group climbed aboard and took three of the four front seats. Tori's mouth hung slightly open at the opulence of the band's existence. Sitting next to her brother, her husband in the seat directly facing her, she tried to relax.

"I'm glad you're here, sis," Brian smiled at her, "Nice to be taken care of..." his voice trailed away before he finished the thought.

Tori smiled without comment, knowing what he meant and well aware of how much being wanted for your assets could hurt.

During the flight, the conversation seemed upbeat.

Tori instinctively inquired about the details and security at the location they were headed towards. "It's in Florida, right? I've been to Miami too many times to count," she giggled a bit nervously. "We won't have any problems there, I hope."

"Yeah, Ft. Lauderdale to be exact, and no, we won't have any problems," Michael explained. "This house is much smaller than the New Jersey estate, only being about seven-thousand square feet, with almost two acres of land surrounding it. There's a full-time gardener and housekeeper, but it's located in a gated community, so there's no security inside the property on a regular basis."

Nodding, Brian added, "We don't take people to our private homes unless they're part of the inside circle. It's better that way... cleaner. There's the community house in New Jersey for parties and such, but otherwise we use hotels."

It felt odd to her, being on the inside circle of her brother's life, but she tried to unwind as the flight continued. Able to catch a small amount of sleep after the stressful last day and a half, Tori and Michael dozed off, leaving Brian to observe them while they slept.

Staring down at her worn makeup, Brian could make out the edges of the scar that crossed her left eye. Thinking about the first time he saw it, he speculated if it bothered her. *I wonder if it could be repaired or removed.* He realized she probably wouldn't care, *she's so tough. Of course, I'm sure a lot of that is an act. I bet she's pretty tender on the inside, like Mike said.*

Glancing across at her husband, *I wonder how these two hooked up.* Neither of the Andersons had seen fit to share much of their history with him or the rest of the band. *They're pretty stuck on each other, though.* He recalled his brother-in-law's tantrum at the thought of her going to New Jersey, and at her own protective behavior towards her mate.

He turned towards the window, recalling his first visit to their home, when he had tried to lure her into his world a little further. *I didn't get my way the first time.*

He knew she had said no, as Michael had said she would, but the path had become less certain. *She said she wouldn't come here, had no use for the lustrous and chaotic life of a rock star... or was it Michael who said that?* Shaking his head, he couldn't remember. *Either way, fate has brought her into it, nonetheless. I'll take what I can get, and if I play my cards right, I'll get it all.* The thought made him smile as he glanced at her features again while she dreamed.

Arriving at MIA, the three were met by the typical limo and driven the thirty-five miles to the lakeside estate. Making it through the checkpoint at the main gate, they followed the divided road in, and Tori observed a long hedge down the center, palm trees on both sides, and the ground covered in grass and large sprouting shrubs. A beautiful place, the realization sank in how different her brother's life had been from anything she had ever experienced.

The car stopped in front of the dwelling, and Michael gathered the couple's bags, carrying them up the wide cobblestone walk. Obviously, the gardener kept himself busy, as the yard was immaculate and Tori instantly felt at ease in the tropical location. Breathing deeply, she felt drawn in and eager to see the inside.

The front door opened into an entry area filled with sunshine in the late afternoon. The entire west wall of the house had been made of glass, some standard and some cubes that allowed the light, but were only translucent. With the wide open design, Tori stood at the front entry for several minutes, allowing herself to take it all in.

A formal type sitting area lay to the left, with a decorative fireplace and mantle halfway down the wall between the front door and the outer wall of glass. It contained a couch and several upholstered chairs with a shag rug on the honey colored hardwood floor that ran throughout the entire structure. The tables, both end and coffee, were glass topped, and stepping further in she could see a large white grand piano at the far end of the extensive room, with a mirror covering the entire far end wall next to it.

Back at the front door, a staircase came right down to the entry area. Not solid, it gave the appearance that it floated on its supports made of thin metal bars. The steps made of slats of wood that matched the flooring of the house, it had no back, so one could peek through and see down the hallway that ran behind it.

To the right of all of this stood an archway that led into the dining room, where a white table with another glass top stood with light wood and white colored chairs. The chandelier was beautiful, yet not as excessive as she had expected, and she noted with another decorative faux fireplace on the far wall.

Moving through the house, Tori began to notice something interesting about her brother and his choice of design. His house may have been extravagant, but it also qualified as simplistic at the same time. He chose bright colors or white often, and the light wood of the fixtures and furniture that reminded her of pine could be found strewn throughout the warm and inviting decor.

Brian smiled at her approval, thinking how different of a feel his place held from her dark choice of colors back in Texas. Taking the staircase that led up from the polished silvery kitchen, they were shown to the bedrooms. Each of the three on the water side of the house had a small patio and sitting area, with a private bath and walk in closet. The two on the back side were much simpler, only having a typical sleeping area with a shared bathroom between them, five bedrooms in all.

The community had been built around a small private lake, and his house came with a private beach that extended about fifty feet in either direction from the large deck and swimming pool that could be seen from the bedrooms above. Peering out over the railing, Tori commented, "You know, I have never been swimming in a pool before. I grew up taking baths in the dirty waters of Brazil. I can hardly imagine it being any fun."

Hearing this, Michael vowed with a grin, "Well, we will be picking up suits and I will teach you about swimming in the civilized world."

Tori had to laugh at the thought, the smile easing the tension that had been hanging over the group since their departure from the hospital in LA. "Only if Brian joins us," she insisted, not wanting to exclude their host.

"Oh, you know that's right," he quickly agreed, "I never miss a chance to enjoy a swim."

Making their way down the final staircase that stood on the opposite end from the entrance, they found themselves in the play end of the house, where a barroom stood on the back side. This room had a red colored theme, complete with red felt on the immaculate pool table, and Tori voiced her appreciation, "You're place is really nice, Danny."

The backside also held a studio, where instruments were set up; guitars, drums and the like. "Does the band come here often?" she felt confused, having thought this had been his private residence.

"No, not really. I enjoy my time here playing all of them with varying degrees of skill. Practice makes perfect, you know." He winked at her, giving her his best smile.

Tori made her way over to the large set of drums, allowing her fingers to glide around the silver rims, listening while he explained, "Collin's actually very good with them. Me, I just like to make a lot of noise."

She grinned mischievously at the thought of his banging away, and then at her trying them herself. *It could be fun, even though I've never held a pair of the sticks before; I would love the challenge.*

"Who plays the piano?" she referred to the large instrument that occupied the living area in the front of the house.

Brian shrugged, "Actually, everyone plays at it, but no one's really brilliant at the monstrosity. It's mostly there for decoration. We use the keyboard whenever we need the sound. Much more efficient and flexible," he indicated the smaller device along the wall. *She really loves music,* he observed, *more than she cares to admit, I think.*

Showing her to the glass side of the house, they found a gym, which gave her a stab of sadness, having given up half her workouts to regain her reproductive abilities. The final room, another play area, contained a ping pong table and white wicker furniture, with two large French doors, one set that led out onto the deck and pool area, and the other on the end of the house that gave way to tennis and basketball courts.

By the end of the tour, she had to admit that his home was extraordinary. *I can see why my humble little place in Texas didn't hold the allure for him that his life did.* Making their way out onto the patio, the breeze almost non-existent, she found the flat calm odd to her considering the wind that had been almost constant in other places she had lived.

At that point, Maria, the housekeeper, appeared and Brian directed her to stock the kitchen for their sabbatical. Taking to the stairs, they chose which room they would be staying in, Tori insisting on having the suite directly next to her brother. Smiling to himself, Brian lumbered into his bedroom to rest, closing the door behind him.

Everyone Wants

Left alone in their suite, she noted quietly, "This one room is almost as large as our entire first house," with only slight exaggeration. Staring out the front glass again, "And this view is truly incredible." Giving him a sideways glance, his eyes were on her, and she grinned.

Smiling, he leaned against the window next to her, arm above his head, "Yeah, nice place. Even better with you here," he teased as he gave his wife a hungry leer, ready to make her scream.

Quick to respond, having gone without for far too many hours, Tori grabbed her husband roughly. She slid her left hand up to hold his neck and run her fingers through his sandy brown hair. Their lips coming together, they kissed one another coarsely, not the least concerned with the open expanse that allowed the evening sun to shine into their room as it sank into the lake.

Pulling at his shirt, she lifted it over his head and ran her fingers through the hairs on his chest, teasing the ones that partially concealed her name. The tickle made her eager and she stepped away from him to remove her clothing. She smiled to herself, happy with his growing ability to throw tenderness aside once in a while and fuck her like mad.

Michael hung back to enjoy the view, opening his

jeans and dropping them out of the way. He loved watching her strip down, her slender form beautiful and her scars invisible in the fading light.

He watched the curve of her hips, noticing she had rounded a bit since she wasn't pushing herself so hard. He admired the way her muscular form had grown not quite as exaggerated, as small deposits of fat had naturally filled in some of the hollows, giving her a more curvy stature.

Her tongue tracing the line of her lips, Tori became taken by the urge to toy with him. She dashed away from him, giggling merrily and swinging her hair back and forth so that the ends danced above the swell of her naked rear end.

Her small black Dragon mark played peek-a-boo with him for several seconds before he caught up to her. Encircling her with his muscular arms, he pressed himself against her from behind and moaned deeply into her hair covered ear.

Reaching around to grab her fur coated flesh, he grasped the mound and used it to push against her roughly. Finding his way into her moist hollow, he knew she liked it that way and did his best to please her.

She squealed as he moved forcefully against her. "Oh my God, Michael!"

He grinned at the sound of her calling his name, and the pair quickly became lost in the rough excitement of their favorite shared past time.

Brian cast a knowing glance at the door to the couple's quarters, then made his way to the center stairway and down into the kitchen below. *Yeah, that was a mistake. I should'a insisted they take the far end of the hall, rather than letting her choose the room right next to mine.* He knew she had done so out of a desire to be close to him, in case he needed anything, and the idea brought a small smile to his lips, despite the sleep he would lose.

Tori became quite attached to me in the month that I lived with her, in their little house. He considered his younger sibling fondly, *she was such a pain in the ass when we were kids.* But now things were different, and her genuine concern meant a great deal to him.

He opened the fridge to poke around, then allowed it to close half-heartedly. *She was dead almost twenty years to the day, so I'm glad that I've got her back, noisy or not. I'd give just about anything to keep her here, and fuck whether her old man likes it. He can go home alone, for all I care.*

"Maria!" he called down the tiny hallway that led to her quarters and waited for her to appear. "Cook us up some grub, eh babe?" grabbing a bowl of fresh grapes to munch on while he waited.

"Si, senor," Maria smiled, accustomed to his whims.

He had heard the faint sounds of their bump and grind die away, and he felt certain they would be joining him shortly for a late night supper. *Fucking always makes me hungry; I can't see why they would be any different.*

A stab of jealousy stung him for a moment as he realized he would like to have what his sister and her husband shared. *After all, that's what everyone wants; to be loved and accepted by the one who cares for them. To have that* one *to share a lifetime with.*

Brian had had no such luck in finding his special girl, and had become content to take as many of them as he could get along the way in his search. He had a voracious appetite for sex, and even in his injured state, the sound of what had been taking place next door made him long for female company.

A short time later the couple appeared. *Yeah, smoke*

ain't the only thing that gives people the munchies. Good sex does, too. He grinned, "Well, nice to see you two are enjoying yourselves," he teased.

Their satiated smiles gave them away, and they were pleased to see the delicious meal of meat and vegetables almost ready. Brian eyed her as she took her seat, and it made Tori's stomach flop, aware he must have heard their commotion. "Yeah, well, we're married; you can't expect us not to have a romp."

Brian laughed, pushing the bowl of grapes towards her to share. "So, what's the plan, besides you two bumpin' uglies?"

Michael laughed at his crudeness, "I'll be taking my bride shopping in the morning, so we can get that swimsuit she needs unless she intends to go naked," he played into the younger man's juvenile behavior.

Brian laughed at the thought, well aware she was the kind of girl who would not bat an eyelash at showing herself to the neighbors and himself if she had a mind to. Nodding in an exaggerated fashion, he agreed to the trip, "Yeah, I have no desire to check out my sister's toys. So, I guess you better get her something to swim in."

"Well, damn. Ya know, I'm not shy about showing off my goods," she teased with a giggle, "But if it makes you uncomfortable, I guess I can play nice."

Michael joined in the laughter, hoping that she had been kidding. *Two weeks of this shit and we're out of here,* he promised himself.

Eating hungrily, the conversation lulled, everyone lost in thought as their situation unfolded with new quandaries to be considered. Reaching the end of their meal, Tori dared to inquire if he had given any thoughts as to how the band would handle the missing member and the ceremony.

"You know, you're gonna miss your best friend's

memorial if we stay here, as I assume he will be buried in Nebraska," she prodded gently.

Shaking his head, he agreed, "Yeah, I know, but we're gonna stay put. I told myself grandpa's funeral would be my last, and I don't feel the least bit guilty about saying my goodbyes from here." His voice almost chipper, he hid how deeply the loss of his friend tore at him on the inside.

"As for the band," he ploughed on, "I'm not sure what Cody and Collin will want to do, but, I for one, think the missing spot will be filled and the band will go on our tour in April as planned."

Pursing his lips, Brian appeared deep in thought. "You know, Collin is as good at playing the drums as he is the bass. And, he's never been shy about his desire take over the spot. It sucks that Chuck is gone, but this may be his chance."

Playing with his fork, "It may come down to his making the switch, as the band could just as easily find a new bass player instead." Staring at his sister while she ate, *or guitar player, and I know just the one.*

Continuing the thought, he sighed audibly. *Unfortunately, she's eager to take care of me, 'cause I need her, but I'm pretty sure they'll be wanting to get back to their home in progress as soon as I'm all healed.* He knew he needed to play it cool if he hoped to succeed.

Giving a faint grin, he chose his words carefully, "The future's pretty fluid at the moment. We'll have to wait and see." As soon as the meal had been finished, he excused himself and made his way upstairs, hoping to be asleep before his overly zealous roommates were able to begin round two.

Alone together in the kitchen, Michael reached for his wife's hand. Lightly stroking the back of it, "Wanna go for a walk?" he suggested, eager to take her away some place private.

Smiling, Tori agreed, "Mhmm, down on the beach?" she laced her fingers with his and led him out the glass front doors and onto the deck.

Following the railing, the couple made their way over to the wide wooden stairs that dropped down to the private stretch of sand that ran around the edge of the lake. Kicking off boots and socks, Tori curled her toes into the cool earth, her white teeth flashing brightly in the moonlight.

"What a night," Michael breathed, taking up a spot a few feet above the water. Dropping onto the ground next to him, the couple leaned against one another, their hands gently probing in the darkness.

Laying her back, her long tresses brushed off to the side, Michael moved half on top of her and stared down into her eyes, watching as they roamed the stars above and beyond him. "What're you thinking?" he asked in a quiet tone and waited for the long pause he knew she would take before giving her reply.

Michael liked that about his wife. *She's always thoughtful in her words and actions, seldom acting too rushed or quickly.* Brushing the hair that caught and floated up in the slight breeze, he watched her lips breathe her reply.

"I'm so grateful that my brother wasn't taken from me."

Nodding his agreement, "Yeah, me too."

Giving her a small kiss, he parted his lips while she caressed the back of his neck, appearing eager for more. The couple took to heavier petting, but he refrained from removing their clothing in a public place. *Damn boats on the lake at midnight,* Michael lamented mentally, easily able to see her disappointment in his choice.

Resting his forehead against hers, he nuzzled deeper into her hair. Holding her left cheek in his right hand, he allowed his thumb to touch the area he knew to be the lower edge of her scar, *I'm such a lucky man.* "When will you be able to see the doctor?" he asked in a quiet voice.

Tori's heart began to thump with excitement. Smiling modestly, "The follow-up appointment has already been set for the first week of February, before my six months of birth control runs out. After the visit, we get to start making real plans."

He gave her an evil grin at the thought of fucking her with the purpose of planting his seed, and he swelled against her thigh. He muttered a low growl, his lips grazing across hers in the dim light.

Driven heavily by deeper desire, he became more willing to risk being seen, and grasped her pants to remove them. An easy task, since she already missed her boots and socks, she eagerly helped him work her denims down in the darkness, trying to move so that they did not draw too much attention from anyone enjoying the night nearby.

Opening his jeans, he only pushed them down far enough to work himself out, and then rolled on top of her to find his way inside her wet hollow. Obviously, making love outdoors excited her immensely, as he slid easily into her folds of flesh, the wet warmth a sharp contrast to the cool air around them. Driving himself against her, Michael finished rather hurriedly, then helped her re-dress.

Having never had sex on the beach before, the couple quickly discovered the unpleasantness sand could cause and soon abandoned their lover's nest to retreat to the shower. Laughing happily as they climbed the stairs, the pair noticed they were making a mess on the floor. It occurred to her how swiftly they could become spoiled to such luxuries as that house and the maid that came with it, along with all the other things that money can buy.

The warm cascade falling over their naked bodies, he

fondled his wife's breast, while his fingers lightly traced the petals that bore his name. She had branded herself, more or less, by choosing to place it there, and in the bright glow of the large incandescent lights, she felt more than happy to be owned by such a man.

Leading her out to lay her down on the luxurious bed, he placed his face against her trimmed hairs and began to search for her hard flesh. He easily pushed her growing excitement, toying with her hidden treasure.

Tori loved the way he did this for her, and allowed him to work her along, her hands and fingers massaging his scalp and hair excitedly.

While his tongue danced against her, causing her to breathe in short heavy pants, she wondered what it would be like to have such a life, where money came easy and left more time for such things as making love. After all, a little more money and a little more time; that is what everyone wants.

Lap of Luxury

Tori needed little convincing to take several of the suits that she tried on, having Brian's credit card in hand. Thinking back to the breakfast conversation, she had been reluctant to accept his paying for things for her in that manner. However, he had insisted, even tossing in that if she didn't spend at least a few grand, there would be hell to pay.

Doing her best to comply with his request, she bought some lighter outfits, as well as the swimwear. Having not worn shorts since she had been inducted into the Dragons, she took the opportunity to buy a few denim pairs. *Jeans or naked, that's how it's been for years.* Not the least bit shy about her smoothly shaven legs that were as equally scarred as her arms, she modeled them for her husband.

"What do you think?" she looked over her shoulder, long hair swirling down her back, to display her rounded rear end.

Tori felt satisfied, seeing the hungry leer in his eyes as they shifted up and down the long length of her. She had chosen a few half shirts that exposed her belly button beneath her full chest and could easily see how her new ensemble put him into an awkwardly visible condition.

"Yeah, those'll do," he teased playfully.

Smiling to herself as she changed back into her jeans,

it made her heart soar that she could evoke such a strong reaction from him, even though they were married. Tori had never had a problem arousing a man, but considering this one loved her for more than what she did in the dark, she felt overjoyed. Taking the items to the counter, she bought them all and set off to locate shoes to match her new wardrobe.

Finding sandals in a variety of colors, she decided to take three pairs, and felt deeply gratified to see that her total expenditures had topped $3K. Surely Brian would be happy with that.

Next, the couple made their way over into the men's department, where Michael needed no encouragement to choose garments that would complement the ones his wife had procured. After all, he would be silly to walk around dressed in boots and jeans when his girl looked so damned cute in her skimpy new outfits. Also taking a couple of swim trunks, he suggested they pick up matching beach towels to wrap up in or lay out on as well.

Eventually, they climbed into the limo that had been stuffed with their acquisitions, and sat leaning against one another as it wound its way back to the house. Seeing the wide grin on his face, Tori thought he looked quite happy, in the lap of luxury. *Why did he resist so hard, when Brian had wanted to bring us into his life more fully a few short months ago?*

Arriving at the house, her brother came out to help them carry the large number of bags inside, eager to peek at their purchases. Tori shyly admitted, "We spent a bit over five thousand," as she produced the plastic to return it.

"Naw, you keep it. It's yours," he laughed at the paltry sum. "And next time, I'll be joining you to show you amateurs how to shop."

After lunch, the group went to change clothes for an afternoon of pool-sitting. Tori dressed in her new white, string bikini, perfectly at ease with having so much of her made public.

Watching her shaking her long dark curls, Michael stared at her, stunned by her beauty. *Maybe we could forget about the pool. I could simply untie her strings in the privacy of our suite,* he thought with a devilish grin.

Downstairs, they spread their towels on the lounge chairs, and he sprawled out with a cold drink in his hand, willing to waste the rest of the day watching her as she moved.

Tori seemed restless, making her way over to dip her toes in the cool water. Not really liking the temperature, she swung her hair around and made quite a production of sitting, and then lying in various locations, allowing the sun to shine down on her and smiling all the while.

Eventually, Michael noticed a group of men over on the balcony of the house next to theirs, and nonchalantly indicated them to his brother-in-law, who languished beside him.

"Oh, them," Brian blew them off easily. "That's the son of a wealthy businessman and a few of his friends. They hang out here pretty much year round, living off the old man's success."

Michael nodded, more concerned about how they seemed quite fascinated with what went on around the pool in front of him rather than their own. He wasn't sure if Tori had noticed them, as she flouted about, but he had begun to feel pangs of jealousy as the men were obviously talking about her as they waved their hands in her direction and were laughing loudly.

The thought of other men being interested in his wife bothered him deeply. Of course, at a distance, he could assume they were unable to see the scars that covered her delicate skin, *like the scars matter. They're simply reacting to the beautiful curves that she's acquired as of late.* Allowing the scene to play out before him, he watched her as she sat with sunglasses on, leaning back with her hands stretched behind her at the water's edge.

Her left leg pulled up with her foot flat on the concrete, her right dangled into the pool. Bent at the knee and flexing it, she kicked the water with her heel. She sat at an angle so that he had a good view of her profile, and as she tilted her head back, her hair fell into a dark silk cascade. Her chest pushed forward, she made a nice silhouette for her fan club across the way.

After Michael's comment, Brian had begun to watch his sister more intently, growing amused as she appeared to be quite into the show she put on for the onlookers. Shifting on the plastic furniture, he leaned closer to the other man and asked in a low tone, "You think she knows they see her?"

His former employee grunted, "Without a doubt."

Rising, a bit angry at the display, Michael made his way over and took a seat to his woman's right, between her and the men who stood gawking at her. She gave him a broad smile and removed her dark shades as he sank down next to her, and he suddenly felt guilty at his distrust of her behavior. Reaching over, he allowed his finger to trace the rose on her chest, it being clearly visible against the white cloth. *Calm down buddy, she's still yours.*

Immediately, she pulled herself up next to him, giving him a deep, open-mouthed kiss while she laid her hand over the back of his for a moment before releasing him. He slid his hand freely over her breast, then down her naked waist to flick the string that hung next to her hip. She cooed that she loved him, and he sneered, realizing maybe for the first time, what a minx she truly was.

Ready to take her upstairs for a generous pounding, Michael could not resist the urge to look back at the group of men who stood quiet and still, watching the couple grope one another. Giving them a quick glance, he waved as he stood and offered his lover his hand.

She grasped his palm lightly, and he helped her to her feet, turning her so that they would have a good view of the show when his hand slid down to massage her round posterior before he took her out of sight.

Once they were safely back in their suite with the door closed, Michael tossed out a snide comment on her bad behavior, "I don't believe I have ever seen you act that way."

Tori's laughter seemed almost evil, and she informed him, "Oh, they can look all they want, my body and soul belong to you."

"Oh, does it," he joined in her dark humor. Grabbing her flimsy attire, he pulled the pieces off of her hastily and turned her around in front of the bed. Standing behind her, he pushed her chest down, causing her rear end to stick out in an exaggerated manner.

Fingering her wet folds, he considered how putting on the display had excited her. Pushing his finger roughly into the pucker of her rear end, she seemed startled by his action, and he grinned that she still had those secret desires to be naughty, which he refused to quell for her.

Dropping his trunks to the floor, he pushed his engorged hardness into her, grasping her hips as he pounded her with a deep, demanding motion, anger still seething inside.

Relishing in his aggressive fucking, she became even noisier than usual, and he paused when the time came to allow the urge to pass, again tickling her wrinkled skin with his thumb and allowing it to drive her panting into quick yelps of desire.

Ready to move within her again, he grasped the flesh of her ribs and hips, squeezing more firmly than he needed to, driven by the urge to punish her nasty thoughts and behavior.

Their bodies thrust together so forcefully, she almost sounded in pain, but he didn't relinquish until he had fully added his own juices to hers, pulling her hair as he did so. Standing behind her, he ran his hand across the small of her back and the roundness of her rear end, clenching his jaw while resisting the urge to leave a handprint on her thigh the way he had seen Red do so long ago.

He trusted she would never willingly be with another man, but the fact that she enjoyed their attention bothered him, and he refused to be tender with her. Instead, he pushed her forward to remove himself and went to wash the smell of her off before dinner.

Abruptly left in the room alone, Tori felt somewhat confused by his behavior. *What the fuck? You mean that's it?* Allowing herself to stretch out on the bed, she listened to the water and considered the man who stood beneath the spray. *He's so odd sometimes,* not like the men of her past who were so easy to read. Eddie had always enjoyed the fact that other men noticed her. Only if she took an interest in them would there be any trouble.

Not Michael, apparently. *He seems pretty pissed off that they were watching me. And he fools around with me, knowing what I want and need, but keeping it from me as if it were some kind of game, torturing me in his own way.*

Her thoughts began to boil as she compared the men from her past with her current lover, placing Enrique in between the two extremes. *He didn't seem at all bothered to share, and he sure as hell proved he could be tender and thrilling by the end.*

Hearing the sound come to an end, she stood and went in to have her own private turn in the shower, her body still on fire, as he had not bothered to satisfy her. Angered by his actions, she did little to hide her disgust when she sauntered into the spacious room.

He picked up on her vibe rather quickly. Running the towel over his soaked skin, he rocked his jaw side to side. "You know, I have to say I was really disappointed." He kept his tone even, wanting to make his point clear without escalating the situation.

"Oh yeah? Me too," she let the words hang for a moment, not looking up and missing his surprised expression before he squashed it.

"You too? What the fuck did *I* do? You were the one prancing about, strutting around like a damn stripper in that skimpy little suit of yours." *Shit, I didn't wanna have a fight.* So far he had done a pretty good job of avoiding them since he had been with her, but not today.

Tori chewed the inside of her cheek, still staring at the sink in front of her, "I'll prance around however I like. You didn't seem too concerned about how I looked when I was buying it!" Her head snapped up to glare at him, eyes flashing blue fire.

"Of course not, I expected you to have some dignity, not flounce around like a harlot!"

Jaw dropped, she rolled her tongue, counting to ten, "You got some nerve, Michael Anderson, and I got news for you – you don't own me, and I will prance, flounce, bounce and strut however the fuck I feel like. Now, get the hell out so I can have a shower." She raised her chin in defiance, her lip quivering as her anger overshadowed her fear.

"Gladly," her mate stormed out of the room, clutching his towel around him.

Beneath the cascade, Tori stared down at her trembling digits. She didn't like to let herself reach that point, where pure rage controlled her. *This isn't good, baby girl. You know better than letting your anger win. And yelling at him isn't going to solve anything.*

Mildly calmer, she exited the bathroom a short time later, to find her mate standing in his jeans, muscled back exposed as he glared out across the water, hands clenched behind him.

"I'm sorry," he spoke before she had a chance to say anything, not daring to look at her.

"For what?" she asked bluntly, her words curt, her anger still on simmer.

He turned enough to smile at her, his hands bouncing lightly. "I'm still a real asshole some of the time," he countered in a playful tone. "This is a hard place for us, love, and I can't wait to take you home."

Curious, she slithered closer to him, still wrapped in her bath sheet, "Hard how? I don't get it. They were just looking. Men always look. That's how they are."

"Yeah," he agreed with a nod, exhaling loudly, "And I know that I don't own you. That's something I treasure about you very deeply… your independence." He looked her up and down, *God she's beautiful. What do I expect her to do, hide inside all day?* "Please forgive me. I'll try really hard not to do that again."

"Do what again?" she queried, suspecting he felt guilty about the way he had manhandled her, pulling her hair and putting things in places he normally avoided.

Nodding, he confirmed her suspicions, "I know you like it rough, but I was outta line. I don't like to treat you that way. I'd rather not touch you at all than do things that hurt you."

Tori grinned, "You know I'm gonna break you of that, sooner or later."

Spying her tiny smile, he smirked with a shake of his head. "Come on, love," he reached out and tugged on her arm, guiding her over to the bed so he could finish her. *Bad girl or not, she's mine, and I'm gonna take care of her, the very best that I can.*

Removing her towel and burying his face where her legs came together, he released a deep sigh, *we're gonna be late for dinner,* not that he really cared.

Rest and Regroup

Having his wife ogled by strangers would only be the beginning of Michael's problems; issues that would test their relationship more than he cared to think about. On the second day after their arrival, Brian had begun to feel much more comfortable, able to get around to an extent, and ready to get back to normal.

After a nice brunch, the trio made their way into the studio, Brian and Tori, drawn by the lure of their shared passion for music and the need to pour their souls into an instrument. With no shortage of variety in the house, she practically bounced around the room, looking them over, before making her choice of which one to try first.

Taking a seat in a straight-backed chair, legs extended out front and arms crossing his chest, Michael could do little to hide his sullen disposition. His wife wanted to explore the new thrills that her brother's collection could afford her, and it took all his effort not to actually scowl at the process and keep his negative commentary to himself.

"Ok, hun, so tell me about these. How do I do this?" she held Brian's sticks and tried to sit on the little stool more comfortably as her husband observed her. Obviously excited, it pained him that he could not share in her joy of the discovery.

"Well, you hold them," Brian patiently slid her hands down towards the backs, "Now, relax your grip... You're choking it... Here, let me show you." He pulled the thin shaft of wood out of her hand and demonstrated. "See? Nice and gentle, almost like it's just lying in your hand."

"Like this?" Tori held up the other half of the set, trying to imitate her sibling.

"Yeah, sort of. You just gotta practice. You'll get the hang of it. Now, allow the stick to bounce, so you're not stabbing at the top." He laughed at her efforts and she smiled in return, happy in the new activity they were able to share.

Michael could feel the jealousy pulling his stomach into knots. *I hope to God he gets better quick.* He found himself giggling through his displeasure as her arms flailed about and her tongue stuck out slightly, *damn, she's so cute at this. I think we need to get her some more instruments when we get home. Maybe pull the ones out of storage and set them up some place.*

"I think I should start with something simpler," she admitted a short time later, realizing it took a lot of coordination to pull off the drums. "I guess I'm not perfect after all!" She smiled broadly, her mood unshakable.

"Yeah well, these are tough, and it's your first try. Maybe later I'll show you something else, like the piano," Brian's voice had grown tired.

"Oh my God, how selfish of me! You're probably ready for a break," she noted the general slump of his body and grasped that he needed to rest. "Let's go change and spend the rest of the day relaxing by the pool."

Glancing over at her husband as she made the suggestion, she had been happy he had at least come into the room, but wasn't pleased with the pout that he wore. *Of course, the pool will put him in an even worse mood,* and she contemplated what the result of that could bring later. She almost relished the idea of what he would do to her when they were alone if it did. *I kinda like it when he fucks angry,* and she smiled at the thought of it.

Having changed and taken up positions out on the deck, Michael noticed the neighbors were observing them as they had the first afternoon. Relaxing into the chaise, he gave himself a pep-talk. *I'm not gonna fall for this. She's a grown woman, and I trust her, and it's ok if they look.*

True to her word, Tori managed to strike all sorts of creative and provocative poses, giving him ample opportunities to work on his possessive thoughts and attitude. Seeing the men watching her activities excited her, and she briefly toyed with the idea of asking her brother to invite them over, before pushing the thought aside. *Better to keep them at a distance, I guess. Too much temptation, really, and I don't want actual trouble.*

The rest of the day passed without incident, and Michael looked her in the eye when he made love to her that evening. Their evening ritual left him feeling exhausted as he reminded himself the entire time to lessen his grip and be gentle with his love. He did not want to give in to those base desires. He would rather not touch her than do that, and he believed in the end that he had been able to do so.

Tori, however, seemed displeased with his performance, thinking that her show would have pushed him into the rough handling he had given her the day before, or at least she had hoped that it would. *Well, it appears I should've invited them over after all; maybe that would encourage him to man up a little in the sack.* She clawed at his back for good measure, hating the feeling that he wasn't giving her what she wanted.

Turning her back on him when he had finished with her, Tori stared out the window and watched the water dancing in the distance. *Why does he always have to be so nice?* He seemed almost dull with the excitement of her brother's world around her. Drifting off to sleep, she couldn't help the feeling that they weren't such a perfect match after all, *even if he thinks we are.*

The next morning, Tori jumped up early and headed down to burn off her excess energy in the gym, surprised that her husband followed quickly behind. Pushing themselves harder than normal, the couple showered separately afterwards and passed on their morning sex, much to the girl's relief. *Thank God, I hate getting all worked up just to be let down.*

Dressed in their new summer attire, the couple made their way down to breakfast with hardly a word. Glancing at his downturned features, Tori tried not to let her mate's moodiness affect her; they only had a short time left with her brother, after all, and she wanted to make the best of it.

Finding Brian already at the table, the housekeeper busy preparing a meal, Tori bent over to give him an affectionate hug and peck on the cheek. Her arms reaching around to hold him from behind, she cooed next to his ear, "So, what instrument are we going to try today?" her voice lilting lightly from her lips.

Brian grinned as he patted the backs of her hands that lay across his chest, "Actually, I hoped we could play guitars today. I thought I might teach you the new album."

Tori grinned, eager to please her older brother in his time of recovery.

Michael, on the other hand, was livid. Biting his tongue, he could hear his blood pulsing in his ears. *He's still conniving, trying to find a way to keep her here. My warning didn't mean shit to him.* Glaring at the other man, their eyes met briefly, and he could see the sneer as the two of them carried on their silent battle over the girl. *This ain't over, asshole.*

Taking a few deep breaths, Michael slid into his seat and played nice, "That sounds like fun. I guess I'll find something to do around here. Maybe go down and hang out by the lake. In case anyone cares to join me." He cut his eyes over at his wife to see what her reaction would be, then feeling a stab of disappointment that she didn't appear to have even heard the comment.

Brother and sister chatted eagerly during the meal, and Michael continued to do his best to be civil. As soon as he had finished, he rose without comment, wiping his face and dropping his napkin on his plate before he made his way out through the game room, onto the deck and down to the beach. Opting not to go upstairs and retrieve the small tube of UV protection, he dropped onto the sand in a partially sheltered spot, and glanced down at his white legs that were typically covered in denim.

Well, this is a fine place to be. This is supposed to be paradise. Nothing to do here that's even remotely fun for me, though. Chuckling to himself, he realized exactly how the guys must have felt, stuck at his place for almost seven weeks. Stretching out on the cool sand, arms behind his head, he drifted off to sleep.

Moving to the studio after the meal, the siblings took no note of the missing member of their party, eager to break out their guitars and have some fun. Showing her the music he had written, Brian seemed a little putout that she could not effectively read it. However, as soon as he played the songs for her, she took over and made what sounded good somehow even better.

Awakening from his nap, Michael discovered that he had been asleep for hours, and the sun had moved far across the sky, and shone down on his bare appendages. Feeling the burn as he ran his hand across them, he cursed under his breath. Moving stiffly, he made his way into the kitchen, where Maria smiled as she produced a bottle of aloe vera gel to soothe his battered flesh.

After applying the sticky lotion, he took the bottle and quietly made his way down the hall to discover what his wife and brother-in-law were currently up to. Peeking into the studio, he could see Tori with a guitar in her hands, and Brian on a bass, the two of them fantastic side by side.

Pursing his lips, Michael bitterly suspected that Brian intended to make the shift, putting Collin on the drums that he had fancied for so long. *Then, he can take over on the bass, permanently. All he has to do is convince the other two guys to accept her, and I lose.*

Internally, Michael knew he wanted to keep her from joining her older brother in his chaotic and lavish lifestyle. At the same time, he wondered why fate seemed to be pushing her in that direction, by throwing her and her brother together again and allowing him to lure her into his life, bit by bit. *I knew this was a bad idea,* he tormented himself, *but what the hell am I gonna do about it?* Of course, he knew the answer; *wait and see.*

Gingerly making his way up the stairs, he left the pair to their magic, feeling a bit forlorn as he stretched out on the bed that the couple shared. Staring at the ceiling, he allowed his mind to wander over the time that they had been together. He had been lying there, the room engulfed in darkness as the sun had set, until Tori burst in looking for him.

"Michael!?!" she called, her voice dripping with panic, and awakening him with a start. Turning, she caught sight of him in his awkward position, trying to block out the sudden burst of light that had flooded the room when she flicked on the switch. "Oh my God! There you are! What the hell are you doing up here? Are you sick?"

"Yeah, sort of. I fell asleep down on the beach, and I got burned," he indicated his lobster red legs in disgust.

Frozen, Tori stood staring at him, her mind whirling between laughter and tears, guilt eating away at her gut. *I didn't even notice he was gone. All day. Not until we sat down for dinner and he wasn't there.* Seeing him in obvious pain shouldn't have been funny, but somehow, she found herself having to stifle the urge to laugh, only half succeeding.

"Why the hell were you sleeping on the beach?" her open palm indicated his injured limbs. "Obviously, you should have known better."

Glowering at her from his half reclined position, Michael felt as if he'd been slapped. *Are you fucking kidding me? All the fawning she does over other people and this is what I get?* "I'm fine!" he snapped. "It's not like I need you to take care of me or anything. Go eat your dinner and fuck around with your brother some more." Rising, he shuffled into the bathroom, trying to hide his agony while closing the door with a heavy slam.

"Fine! I will!" she shouted through the closed portal, slamming the outer exit to punctuate her words.

Stomping down the stairs, Tori could feel the color rising to flush her face in anger. Flopping down in her seat in the kitchen, she allowed a loud burst of air to escape her clenched jaw. *Son of a bitch. I can't believe he let himself get burnt and then gets all pissy with me about it.*

Mouth open slightly, Brian asked in a quiet tone, "Everything ok?" He had heard the door demonstrations and suspected that it wasn't.

"Yeah, it's fine," Tori lied flatly, then seeing her brother's expression, it occurred to her that it had been pointless to do so. Drawing another cleansing breath, she worked to calm herself. "Michael didn't use any sunblock and let himself get burned today, so he probably won't be joining us. Maybe we should send Maria up with a tray for his dinner."

"Yeah, we can do that." Glancing over at the pretty brunette who hovered nearby, he nodded at the request and she began to prepare a plate for the newly injured man's meal. Switching to their French, he tried to keep the family business private, "Are you ok? I mean, you seem really upset over a little sunburn."

Looking up at his crystal blue eyes, Tori felt torn. She hadn't told her brother how badly her husband disapproved of his lifestyle or her being there to share it with him. Staring, she considered what she should say, if anything, suspecting that her sibling already knew. "He isn't happy here," she finally confessed, with a stab of shame that she had spoken to him so insensitively.

"Yeah, I got that. He huffs around like he's the only one that matters," Brian vented his own frustrations.

Tori pushed her food around on her plate, "I know, and I don't really know what to do about it. But listen, I don't want that to ruin our time here, you know? I mean, when you're all better, he and I will go home." Her eyes flicked up to watch his expression, not even sure if she still wanted to.

Brian's Adam's apple moved as he swallowed, "Yeah, I mean you're only here to take care of me, right? You have a life back in Texas, after all." He smiled, forcing himself to keep a straight face.

"Right!" she nodded, relieved that he seemed to understand.

Finishing their meal, the pair made their way back to the studio for a couple more hours before Tori finally insisted on going to bed. Finding the light off in their room, Michael sprawled and uncovered, she did her best to be quiet as she stripped down and curled up on her side. Being careful not to touch him, she pulled the blanket up to her chest with her back to him.

Lying in the darkness, she couldn't decide what she felt more, guilt or anger. *I should have been more concerned about him,* she reprimanded herself one minute. *But fuck me, he's a grown man, he don't need me to take care of him!* she mentally screamed the next. She continued the debate until she fell into a fitful sleep.

Downstairs, Brian hobbled about setting up a few things for the next time they played together. *Gotta be careful about this,* he warned himself. *Don't want her to know I made this.* But getting her when she wasn't aware was the key, *that way she comes across being herself.* Everything in place, he turned in as well, eager to get some rest for a new day.

Soul Searching

The three continued to share time out in the pool as well as down along the beach in the late afternoons and evenings, and Tori's fan club always seemed eager to take in the show. This, combined with his brother-in-law's perceived plotting, put Michael in a foul mood the better part of the time. His burn took several days to heal, but he pretended it didn't bother him the best he could, using it as an excuse to avoid physical contact with his wife of any kind.

Tori noticed her husband's withdrawal of affection, horrified it had lasted over a week. *Guess I'm back to being a filthy whore,* she felt confident his jealousy reigned supreme. *Well, fuck him if he can't take it.* Becoming moody herself, she put her time and effort into her brother, tending to his needs and spending time in his small studio making music, which she loved.

She thoroughly enjoyed the new songs the group had written, and played them for hours until she could perform them just the way Brian wanted them to sound. The pleased smile on his face made her happy inside, despite her growing turmoil at her husband's odd behavior.

Sitting at dinner after ten days of awkward silences and hurt feelings, she didn't think things could get any worse, when her brother spoke up unexpectedly. "I think it may be time to head north," Brian commented with a half grin.

Tori only stared, wide-eyed disappointment that their holiday would be coming to an end. "You gonna be ok? I mean, you need me to go with you?" she prodded gently.

"Sure!" his voice squeaked slightly, "I mean, yeah, if you wanna come. You're always welcome, you know." He cut his eyes over at Michael, well aware he wouldn't be happy if they did. "But, I think your old man would rather pass on that," he sneered slightly for a moment as he challenged her mate to speak up.

Michael chewed his bite slowly, refusing to take the bait, "Whatever you two decide is fine by me."

Brian's smile lessened a bit, disappointed he didn't get a rise, "Actually, I spoke to the guys, and they're ready to meet. So, we're heading to New Jersey tomorrow. At least I am." He let the statement hang, putting the ball in their court, so to speak.

Tori watched him, then dropped her gaze for a moment, again feeling like a piece of rope being pulled at both ends, and angered by her husband's lack of affection. "Hey, Danny; let's see how you feel tomorrow, ok? Maybe we'll come along." *I'll go if I want to, and if cry baby don't like it, he can go home.*

The couple had scarcely been on speaking terms for days, going to bed each night with him facing the wall, while she stared at the glass and the stars beyond. Spinning his ring with his thumb, Michael chastised himself, *you're gonna lose her if you're not careful. She loves him, too, and you can't ask her to pick between you. That's never a good idea.*

He recalled the day he had told Brian he would win in such a fight, but now he wasn't so sure, and didn't really want to find out. "Yeah, maybe tomorrow we can decide," he quietly agreed with his wife.

Finishing the meal in silence, the group broke up to go their separate ways, each of them lost in thought. After a bit more soul searching, Michael was struck with the idea that they had gone to bed with this issue between them too many nights already, and he needed to make peace.

Finding her on their balcony looking out over the lake as the sun sank into it, he moved in close but resisted the urge to touch her. *Well, this is silly, what the hell are you afraid of? She's your wife, after all.* But he knew she wasn't happy with him, her anger radiating from her for days.

Shifting his gaze from the sunset before them, he took in her profile. "You know, I trust you completely. I hope that you know that, at least." He could see the stiffness of her body as he prepared to grovel. *Damn, this is harder than I thought it would be.*

"What's that supposed to mean?" she frowned, crinkling her nose, "Have I done something else to make you think that you shouldn't?"

Inhaling deeply, he shifted his gaze back to the water, and the red streaks dancing across it. "No, love, it's not you. And this's really hard for me." *Damn, now I look like a dick no matter which way I go.* Deciding at the last minute to cop out and go with the jealousy excuse, he continued, "We've been here almost two weeks, and I see those guys still watching you. All I want to do is take you home." *At least the part about going home is true.* He drew a deep breath, pushing it out through his nostrils loudly.

"And?" she clipped the word, anger below the surface.

At his failure to reply, she tried again. Giving him an incredulous laugh, she hissed in a low voice, "You have got to be kidding me. That's really what has had you so fucking moody? Baby, you know I love you. I chose you, to go home to you, to be with you. I don't understand why it bothers you so much. What should I do, cover myself completely and avoid being seen?"

"I'm not sure it would help, even if you were covered. You're quite a looker, ya know." He paid his love the compliment with a genuine smile, and hoped it soothed any hard feelings over his behavior the last few days. "I just need a little patience, until I learn how to let them look, and not get all bent out of shape about it. Let me take you home." *God please, let me take you home.*

Tori shook her head again, "Bent out of shape doesn't sound like trust. And running back to Texas isn't going to fix that." She scoffed, "You're pretty silly, ya know that? But if it helps, I have no intention of lying with another man, so long as we both shall live."

She felt angry, at him for pushing her, and herself for allowing him to, and tired of hearing that he wants to go home. She had begun to like it there with her brother close at hand, and having him trying to tear her away from it wasn't helping.

Noticing Brian down below them, Tori could see he looked much healthier and rested. Ready to make his way to New Jersey to regroup with the other members of his band, she knew he didn't really need her anymore. Glaring back at her husband, she inquired, "How much longer are you going to allow me to stay with him?"

Her words stung, implying ownership once again. Shaking his head at the stupidity of her question, he heaved another sigh. "We'll stay for as long as you feel the need to stay." He said the words, but wasn't happy with that choice, having expressed the desire to leave, and he could see her brow wrinkle further in disbelief.

"I mean it, love. We stay as long as you need to. You wanna go north with him, we go." He caressed her back, leaning in so that his face lightly brushed hers, trying to ease the tension between them. He had grown tired of the debate, no matter how badly he wanted to avoid going to New York.

"Then it's settled," she replied stiffly. "We can go with him to the house in New Jersey, at least for a few weeks. I want to make sure he's going to be ok." She eyed her mate, deeply saddened by his possessive behavior, and yet angry at the same time. For the first time in weeks, she had felt the doubt creeping in, forming questions in the back of her mind.

Rock and Roll

The next morning, Brian convinced the pair to leave all of their summer clothes in the closet and drawers as the room was officially theirs. He appeared extremely satisfied at seeing his sister's things as part of his home, and hoped they would be a permanent fixture now that she had been drawn in.

Arriving in New York via the private jet, Michael dared to take his wife's hand as they rode in the car. She allowed the gesture with a sullen glare, her grasp not firm enough to imply true comfort. When the limo pulled up in front of the entrance, she removed her palm from his and clasped her hands together rather than return it.

Yup, she's still pissed. Michael eyed his wife carefully as they made their way inside. *You know, you could just tell her the real reason you want to take her home,* he rationalized with himself. *Of course, if I do that, I have to admit that I think she'll fold here.* Running his fingers through his dark curls, he heaved a heavy sigh. *I can't do that to her. I have to let her make the choice.* He only hoped that she would choose him.

Distracted by the warm welcomes of Collin and Cody, he put on his best smile, "Hi, guys! Glad to see you two lookin' good."

Taking his hand to shake it vigorously, "Hey Mike," Collin returned the jovial grin. "Glad to be seen. Hi Tori." He nodded at the girl, ready to play his part in Brian's little scheme. "If you'll follow me, I'll show you two to your room," the bass player curled his fingers as an indication that they should, and the couple lagged behind him up the stairs.

"Is everything set?" Brian leaned closer to Cody and spoke in a lowered tone, his eyes trailing the line of his sister as she reached the top of the staircase.

"Yeah," Cody agreed quietly, "You sure this is what you wanna do? I mean, Mike'd take good care of her. Loves her a lot, ya know? We convince her to join the band, it may put an end to their relationship."

Brian cut his eyes over at his longtime friend, "Yeah, this's what I wanna do. She's a musician, man. Did you listen to the disk?" his eyes narrowed.

Cody inhaled deeply, pushing the air out through his lips loudly, "Yeah, we did. And you're right, she's good. I don't know if outstanding is warranted, but she would be good enough, yes."

Brian rolled his tongue, taking in the man's words, "High praise. Trust me, she's fantastic. Better than me on my best day. You'll see, once we get her to playing with us. But we gotta be suave, ya know? Can't go in guns blazing. That would spook her and he wins."

"He wins. You make it sound like a competition, man." Cody grimaced.

"It is. And she's the prize. If he wins, all her talent goes to waste. You saw where he wants to keep her, that tiny one-horse town. Rebuilding motorcycles? Come on!" he scoffed at the couple's simple life. "That's not where she belongs," his voice began to rise as he pointed at the floor. "She belongs here, with me, making the sounds that put that smile on her face. Ya get it?"

"Yeah, we get it," the singer's words were soft as he nodded his reply. "I only hope you're right about it."

"I am," the taller man beamed with confidence. "Collin gets to play the drums, like he wants, I get to play the bass, like I want, and Tori gets to have the life she shoulda had. Or woulda had if those assholes hadn't taken her and fucked it all up." Turning, he headed down the hallway calling loudly, "Anything to eat around here? I'm starving, God dammit!"

Reaching the refrigerator, Brian began rummaging around, looking for something to snack on. "Stella!?! Where's lunch, babe!"

The older woman, who took care of the kitchen, made her appearance, "Well, look who made it home." She smiled at the third remaining member of the band. "Have a seat, hun, and I'll make ya some grub."

"Grub," he mocked her, "I hope it's not worms this time!" He smiled at their familiar banter, glad to be back in his safe surroundings. "Probably should make enough for everyone. The three of us had an early breakfast before we left Florida."

Making his way over to the window, he stared out into the wide expanse of the yard, his mind still turning over the conversation with Cody. *Yeah, I'm sure, this is where she belongs. I have to be patient; she'll choose it, and I won't have to do anything to make that happen. She wants this.*

Taking a large bite out of a shiny red apple he had pulled from the cooler, he chewed loudly and waited for lunch to be served. "Everything set for tomorrow?" he asked the cook absently.

"Yes, sir; you'll have a fine feast tomorrah," she grinned. "A Thanksgivin' dinner t' remember."

"Good," Brian nodded to himself. *Everything's falling into place.*

Collin had led the couple on a tour of the house, mostly for Tori's sake after they had been presented with their quarters. Finishing the loop, the trio entered the spacious kitchen to the smell of cooking burgers with all the trimmings.

Tori smiled to herself, *I could sure get used to having meals ready on demand, that's for sure.* The thought immediately produced images of Trish and the diner and a guilty twist in her gut. *But what I have at home isn't bad either,* and for a moment, her anger at her mate ebbed. *Damn.*

Sidling up next to her brother, she crossed her arms, "What ya' lookin' at?" she adopted her southern drawl.

Giving her a quick glance and dropping an arm across her shoulders, still chewing the fruit, "Nuthin. Thinking it's gonna be winter any time now, an' we need to get you guys geared up for that. How 'bout a shoppin' spree? My treeaat." He smiled broadly, singing the word treat to entice her further.

Tori chuckled lightly, "Sure, Danny; I guess we can do that," eager to spend time with her brother. *Eventually, we'll have to go home, it's only a question of when,* but she opted not to push the issue.

Eager to give her more roots in his world, Brian took his sister and brother-in-law out as soon as they had eaten. Hitting New York's most famous districts, Michael couldn't help feeling like an outsider, watching the siblings as they laughed and talked, picking out clothes and sharing stories.

They're getting along, let them enjoy each other, he reminded himself as he pretended to be choosing shirts. But deep down, he felt as if his wife was being taken from him, piece by piece. *I've always given her plenty of room; hopefully not so much I let her get away.*

It only took them a few hours to fill the massive closet with a variety of new clothes adapted for all types of winter scenarios, much to Michael's dismay. *Like we need all this shit.*

Surveying the new wardrobes with hands on his hips, he squinted in disgust. *So much for going home before Spring. I'll be lucky to get her back there in time for her appointment come February.* The thought saddened him a bit, *I forgot about that. Why did she get my hopes up about having a family if she didn't really want one?*

Noting the girl getting ready for bed, he muttered under his breath, "I think I need to sleep in another room," and walked out in disgust.

Tori stared after him, mouth wide open in surprise. *What the fuck? My God, he acts like a damn child!*

Left alone, Tori put on some sleep shorts and climbed into the king sized bed. She wondered briefly where he had ended up, and considered going to locate him, if only to have her say about his continued insensitive behavior.

Instead, she lay in the dark and toyed with her ring. *He's really pissing me off. And I didn't even do anything to deserve this shit.* Pulling the band off completely, she laid it over on the nightstand, staring at it as she drifted off to sleep. She used to think they were in love, but lately she wasn't so sure.

Waking up in a cold sweat before sunrise, Tori struggled to slow her breathing as her heart pounded loudly inside her chest. She rolled over to find the ring still lying on the small table. *What a fucking nightmare!* She had dreamt the ring was gone, the panic and search that followed bringing feelings of intense fear crashing in around her.

Grasping the symbol of her husband's devotion, she squinted at the words engraved inside before sliding the band into its proper position. Forming a fist several times and watching the ring as she did so, *I really need to work on being a better wife,* she reproved herself. *I can't lay all of the blame for this on him. But, how the hell am I going to fix it?*

She recalled the times her husband had tried to talk to her as of late, and she had snubbed him. *Or come across with cheeky responses. Damn, how could I be so stupid?* It was Thanksgiving Day, and she knew he would have to see her, as dinner had already been planned, *so at least he won't be able to avoid me completely.*

Of course, Michael being her first and only experience at maintaining a relationship, she was bound to make a few mistakes. Climbing out of bed, she dressed and primped, ready to make things right with her lover, *if it's not too late. God, I hope it's not too late,* and she sniffed at the sadness the thought of losing him brought her.

Later that morning, the holiday meal turned out nice enough, despite the conflicting ideas and ambitions within the group. The cook prepared a fabulous turkey dinner, and the guys all gathered around the extravagant dining room table to feast upon it.

Michael had continued to avoid his wife, and she had allowed him to do so, still not sure what she would say, fully aware that she had been pulled between two worlds once again. *I know what I want; I have to figure out how to get it.* Embarrassed about her behavior, she could see a great deal of sucking up in her near future.

Sitting down to loaded plates, Tori noticed that hardly anyone spoke, which left her with the entire meal to observe and consider each point of view.

It turned out, her husband had become increasingly easy to read, his deeply wrinkled features making it all too clear; *he really is unhappy, and all he wants is to go home.* He pushed his food around on his plate, not eating nearly enough of the delicious meal, the sight of it almost enough to send her packing in itself.

Her brother also seemed exceedingly simple to

understand, the way he smiled and doted on her. *He never has given up on my living with him.* The thought made it even more evident; *I really don't belong in this house, even if the visit has been comfortable enough.*

Observing the remaining two members of their small party, she wondered how they felt in the midst of all of this. *Collin has been sweet as honey since we arrived. Guess he got over my refusing his advances after all. Or maybe he is playing nice for Danny's sake; maybe they both are.*

She appreciated that they both cared for him, and that brought her some degree of comfort. *He won't be totally alone, and he'll still have friends to look out for him after we're gone.*

"Wow, this group isn't usually this quiet," she broke the silence with a loud voice. Smiling, she tossed a bone to see who would snatch it up, "Better talk it up guys. Michael and I will be leaving Sunday, after all."

Her husband's head popped up at her words, his heart pounding, "We are?" His voice squeaked slightly, and he cleared his throat to cover himself, "I mean, we are. Yes."

Brian was not amused, "But I just bought you guys a closet full of clothes for the winter!" His disappointed expression could not have shown through any clearer, any more than the relieved ones that Cody and Collin wore. If she left, they were off the hook as far as letting her join their band.

Twisting her fork, Tori remained calm, "Yeah, baby; I know. And we really appreciate that. I bet you can return all that stuff if you want. It was a lot of fun, being out, spending the day with you and all. And maybe we might come back for a visit in time to use some of them…" her voice trailed away as she reached the part about leaving. "But we don't belong here, and we're only kidding ourselves if we ever thought otherwise."

Jaw dropped in disbelief, Brian's mind raced. "You're serious? Just like that? What if I need you to take care of me some more?"

His sister laughed out loud, "You're fine, you don't need anyone to take care of you." She looked down at her plate, "We want to have a family. And to do that, I need to go home." Not giving anyone else a chance to speak, she rose from her chair and headed up the stairs.

Family Always Wins

"What the fuck just happened here?" Collin blurted out, holding up open palms in awe.

"I think, they're leaving," Cody supplied, still chewing as he spoke.

"Yeah, no shit, Sherlock, I got that part," the new drummer snarled, "But what the hell? One minute you guys are happy, eating this shit up, and the next you're running off back to Texas? What kind of game is this?" He glared at her partner while making his demands.

Michael shifted in his seat, uncomfortable at the part he had played in his wife's sudden change of heart. Clearing his throat, he made a small apology as he stared at the door, "I think it may be my fault. I never really wanted to come here, or stay here that is. I've been putting some pressure on her to go home, more or less."

"There you go with that more or less bullshit again," Brian spoke up, "So what did you say to her?"

Michael rocked his jaw side to side, studying his brother-in-law intently, "Don't really matter, does it? She's *my* wife, and if we want to go home, we go home. End of story."

Slamming his fist down on the table, "The hell if it don't, jackass. She may be *your* wife, but she's *my* sister, and blood is damn sure thicker than water!"

Upstairs, Tori could hear their voices raised; the shouting echoed through the massive structure. Deep down, she knew that was the reason she never wanted to come to the house in the first place. *I didn't want to choose... I didn't want to have to choose between them.* She would never be able to take a side, and it wasn't fair for them to ask her to, as she had felt them silently pulling on her since Brian first suggested it, back in Texas.

Now they were there and she felt stuck, like being in the center of a tug-of-war, playing the part of the rope. *No matter which way I go, someone I love gets hurt.* Leaning on the glass, pressing her forehead against the cool pane, she stared out across the wide yard filled with the colors of fall. *God, I need a drink.* And then she realized she knew where she could get one.

Turning away from the picturesque scene, she scurried to the far set of stairs, away from the dining room where the small group of men still exchanged insults. Intending to hit the bar in the lounge, she snaked her way down the hall. Passing the studio lined with instruments, she stopped cold. Spying her brother's guitar, she had another idea. A wonderfully wicked idea.

Moving into the room, she grabbed the neck of the device, prepared to smash it in her fit of rage. Holding it, she stopped, paralyzed in thought. *This's the guitar that Terry built!* The memory of her former mentor flooded her brain, clouding her destructive purpose. *He cared so much for me.* As if she could feel the love he poured into his creation pulsing in her hands, *I can't smash Terry's guitar...* The hot tears on her face, she felt more alone than she had in over a year.

Caressing the finely polished shine, she lifted the apparatus to her, overtaken by the strong desire to play it, rather than destroy it. She wanted to make it talk, to cry out with the flow of pain. *My pain. The pain no living person can ever understand...* Throwing the strap over her shoulder, she plugged in the amp and allowed her fingers to slide across the strings.

She started with *Nobody's Angel*, allowing the song to flow out of her, replaying her special riff several times at the end to emphasize her control over her life and her destiny. *Nobody owns me, nobody uses me, nobody anymore...* Her raw anger spent on the lengthy display, she became calm, feeling the rush wash over her, and she moved on.

She went through her spiral of songs, her mind turning the pages. She played them as if it lay before her, piece after piece. Lost in her secret place, the one that her soul created when her fingers brought a guitar to life, her hair fell over her face and she drifted into another world, and this one of flesh and blood quickly faded into oblivion.

Having heard the noise over their angry confrontation, the group of men stood in the doorway of the studio. Hovering together, the three band members were in awe, while Michael wore a satisfied smirk. He had watched such displays many times in their home, and he knew the peace she would feel when it was over.

Lost in her completion, and the instrument that conformed to her very being, she took no notice of the four men who had moved from the entrance into the room. She had reached the end of her book, and her fingers ran through simple chords.

Her mind turning, she began to play the album, the guys' album that her brother had taught her in Florida. She knew how he wanted the songs to sound, but she didn't care. She would play his song, only this time she would butcher it, carving out its heart and offering it to the gods.

Hearing the altered riffs, Brian moved to stop her, but

Michael caught his arm. "No, man; let her play. It's beautiful... I promise." Jerking his arm away, Brian stood with the others, still fuming, like he had done in LA the first time he heard her tearing apart his hard work.

Within a few minutes, she hit upon the sound she wanted, and she began to sing, having chosen the piece whose words moved her the most deeply. Her tone perfect, her voice brought chill bumps as she played the song that she had taken and made her own.

A few minutes later, the men stood dumbfounded as the amp fell silent. Bringing her fingers to her forehead, the girl caught her long black tresses, running her digits against her scalp and tossing the mane behind her. Opening her eyes, she took the group in calmly from her place of serenity.

"Wow," Collin muttered aloud, his eyes darting back and forth between the two people that mattered more to her than anything else on earth. "I guess I see your dilemma. But in the end, you gotta choose what's right for you. You do that; you tell both these guys to go fuck themselves, and you go join a band."

"Yeah," Cody agreed, "Or you could join ours." Collin shot him a surprised look, but he shrugged him off, "What? She's good enough. We'd be lucky to have her!" After all, that was the plan, even if that wasn't how it should have gone down.

Taken completely off guard, she stared at the trio. *There's no way they're offering me a spot in their band.* Her mind swirling memories of the past few weeks and her brother's behavior, she was angry all over again. *Son of a bitch, he intended this!*

She was pissed that he had tricked her, in a roundabout way, meaning to try and persuade her to do precisely that. And even more pissed at the world because she knew she could never accept such a position. Stomping out of the room, Tori felt defeated.

Brian swallowed hard, causing his Adam's apple to bob up and down. He knew he was close to getting his way, and he grinned at his bandmates, "Give her a few minutes, she'll come around."

Taking Michael in with an ice cold stare, he contemplated how he had hurt his friend deeply with his plotting and deception. *But it don't matter, this is family,* he thought to himself with a wry grin, *and in the end, family always wins.*

In her room, Tori's fingers trembled as she grabbed her backpack and threw in the few items they had brought with them, having no intention of taking the new clothing back to Texas with her. *How could I have been so stupid? Why didn't I see this coming?* She chided herself, angry at allowing her brother to draw her in. *And the problems this has created between Michael and me! Oh my God, I'm so ashamed.*

Hot tears stained her cheeks as she thought about her husband and the hurt she had caused. *How will I ever make this up to him?*

Her thoughts continuing to tumble, the girl knew there would be no way she could accept such a public position. She no longer feared her old life, as she had dealt with the Dragons and Scorpions; *it's unlikely anyone would be looking for me.*

That being said, it would be madness to put herself out into the public eye, not knowing who might see her and put her together with some past incident. *It would be folly to think I could go unnoticed by everyone who might recognize me and try to pull me back into my old life, for one reason or another.*

Hearing a light rap at the door, Tori paused briefly, standing still to await her visitor's interjection into her muddied thoughts. After a lengthy gap, she lifted her gaze to find Brian staring at her, his eyes wide with concern at her contorted features.

Drawing a deep breath, she blurted, "I can't play in your band, Danny. I'm sorry you thought that I would ever consider it, but I can't put myself out there like that. It would put everyone I care about in danger."

Shaking his head, he countered, "That's not good enough. If you don't wanna play with us, that's fine, but you're gonna have to have a damned good reason. Everyone sees what the music means to you. Everyone but you."

Turning her palms towards the ceiling, she emitted a disgusted tone, "They don't even like me, why would you put yourselves through such a thing?" She ignored the truth behind his words, "Just let me go, please!"

"Alright, you can go. But only after you come downstairs and explain to everyone why you feel you have no place among us. Because, quite frankly, this is where you belong. Playing that guitar is the thing that brings you to life. It makes you a star, even when you're not on stage. You love it, and you're God damned good at it," he clamped his hands together, shaking them in front of himself towards her as if to pray, "Why can't you see it?"

His eyes searched for a sign she understood. Seeing none, he went on, "Look, you wanna go hide in Texas and play wife, working on motorcycles and run down houses, that's your business. But first, you have some explaining to do."

Trying to send him away, she realized her older brother could be as equally stubborn as she could. *Fuck me, if I don't do this, I could lose him, as if he had been the one who died.* Unable to take that risk, she had to make him understand. Following him downstairs, an angry scowl marred her beautiful features, and she fumed every step of the way.

Finding the rest of the group in the kitchen setting leftovers on the table, the five of them took their seats. Tori sat, too anxious to eat, and fully aware that she would soon embark on sharing the story she had not intended to tell anyone ever again.

Looking across at her husband, he gave her a small smile and spoke to her in German. "You don't have to tell them. I'll back you if you want to say *no* is your final word and walk away."

Her eyes flitting from one face to the next, she realized she could probably get away with such a course of action, but it would cost her dearly in her relationship with her brother. She wanted to have him in her life, even if she couldn't stay with him, and to maintain that, she would have to be willing to concede some parts of her past to them.

Outlaw Days

Staring at her plate, Tori tried to decide how to begin the conversation. Shaking her head, she shared the German for a moment, her voice quiet as she replied, "I really can't do that. I owe him this much." Her eyes taking him in, she breathed a small sigh of relief; *at least he's back on my side.*

"So," she switched to English for the benefit of everyone in the room, "You think you're ready to hear about my outlaw days? Well then, let me warn you. You cannot un-hear what's been said. Search your hearts and be sure this is what you truly want, as my tale will be dark, and we all may live to regret it." Her voice dripping with ominous foreboding, she cut her eyes around the gathering, waiting for them to indicate their agreement to the terms.

Her words gave the three band members chills, as they considered her lack of emotion at their utterance. To convey his agreement, Brian gave her a single nod, "Yeah well, we spent all that time hiding at your place in Texas, so it's been pretty obvious that you were involved in some pretty bad shit. The least you can do is tell us yourself, and not leave us hanging with the little amount your old man was willing to share."

On the inside, Tori allowed herself a small smile at having Michael referred to as her *old man*. On the surface, she held her face placid, unwilling to show any inward sensitivity.

Feeling the need to make her brother understand how deep and dark her past truly was, she started with her first memories; the day both their lives were changed. She had shared them with Brett, connecting the two of them forever, so they were fresh in her mind, so to speak.

"I guess you know I have slowly regained memories of my life before the Dragons. Not only of us playing together, or rather me chasing you around, such as it were. I remember the day we left you at the farm," she gave a pause, indicating the day their parents were murdered.

Brian raised his eyebrows at her, "Wow, you were pretty young. How do I know you actually remember it, and not just me talking about it?"

Seeing that he wanted something more tangible than her word, "Oh, I don't know, I guess I've always found it odd that they chose to paint their barn green, rather than the traditional red."

Upon hearing this, he nodded, having been supplied with the right detail, and knew she did indeed remember their grandparent's farm.

"After we left you, I was busy being angry. I guess you had noticed I never liked not getting my way, and we stopped at a diner for an early dinner. Mom and dad promised me a treat to cheer me up. Only, a couple of rough guys in leather came in. Mom didn't like the look of them, so we left. One of them had touched me on the head, and she freaked."

"I knew I wasn't getting my prize, so I started throwing another fit in the backseat." A tear dropped onto her cheek before she could catch it, and she sniffed slightly, willing herself not to cry.

"Mom pulled my bear out of my bag, trying to get me

to quit carrying on while dad was driving. Like you can talk sense to a five year old." Tori grinned slightly at her own misbehavior.

"She saw something out the back glass, and she screamed before we were hit and spun off the road. I dreamt it lots of times after that."

Michael nodded, having recalled their sharing before she took his name.

"They put me on a motorcycle, and I heard the shots before they set the fire." She held her face of stone, daring her brother to show emotion at how their parents died. "The bike was scary, as I sat facing the guy, hanging on for dear life, and I was cold with the wind whipping around me."

"I have no idea how far we went. We stopped at a gas station and I was taken into the bathroom by one of the guys, where he stripped me and gave me a new set of clothes to put on, which I refused."

"It was Eddie Farrell, leader of the group, and he laughed at me. Grabbed my arms and forced the shirt on over my head and the pants onto my legs. Then he snarled at me, '*Now, your new name is Tori. Tori Farrell. If anyone asks, that is all you are allowed to say.*' He poked me in the chest and must have thought I would be afraid of him..." Her voice trailed away for a moment, her rubbing the spot as if she could still feel the digit stabbing her small body.

"But I wasn't afraid of him and kept telling him my name was Nikki. Nikki Peters. Each time that I said it, he hit me. But I wouldn't stop and he wouldn't stop, so he hit me harder and harder, until we were interrupted."

"Another guy came in and told him the clerk was outside listening to him beat me. Eddie pointed at me, and told him to fix it or they would have to dump me."

Brian wore a shocked expression as the meaning of the words *dump me* sank in.

"There was something... special... about the way Henry had looked at me. His eyes were a deep brown, and he knelt down on the bathroom floor in front of me and said, *'Listen, baby girl. Ya have t' use yur new name now. If ya don', things are gonna end badly fur ya. I'm gonna take care o' ya if ya let me, but ya can't make Eddie mad like that. He'll take ya away from me if ya do.'"*

Michael smiled at the way Tori imitated his brother perfectly.

"He used paper towels to clean my face. He told me his name, Henry Morgan, and he shook my hand. When Eddie came back, he said we were good and I rode with him after that, hanging on to his chest and wrapped in his jacket." Looking over at her husband, she felt moved by his expression as she described his brother, a story he had never heard.

Her eyes shifting back to her sibling, Tori waited for him to contemplate that portion of her account, hoping it had been enough to satisfy his need to know. On the contrary, it only left him wanting more, and as the pause grew extended, he made a circular motion with his right hand. Taking this as an indication to go on, she continued, her voice almost mechanical.

"I'm not sure where all we went from there, but we ended up down in South America, at a camp the guys had. It was a vast location, in the heart of the jungle..." and she described her childhood home for him in detail. She had shared pieces of her life there with Brian, but she knew the other guys wouldn't know.

Elaborating about the early arrangement of the group, she explained how the majority of them only came and went from the camp, while Henry and three others stayed on full time and took on the majority of the work in raising her. She explained how Brian Turner had started off training her right away, and how she had been taught how to read, do math, and given lessons so that she became fluent in all five of her current languages.

Reaching the part of her early teens, she explained how Eddie began to grow more distraught, returning to the camp to find she had physically changed little since his departure. "He was waiting for me to go into puberty," she elaborated, "Which confused me. I wasn't sure what it was all about, or why it mattered."

Brian's eyes grew wide, still a bit surprised they had waited, but knowing what was coming when it finally occurred. "How old were you, when it happened?"

"Uh, seventeen or so my doctor guesses. And by that time I had grown to love Henry so deeply. He refused to touch me though. He was saving me for Eddie. And, after I finally began to mature, Eddie and the rest remained in the camp and finished off my training for about two more years before it was decided I was ready."

Taking another long pause, Tori blinked at him for a moment, closing her eyes to calm herself, and then began to explain about what happened between the two of them the last night she shared Henry's hammock. Not waiting for a response, she continued on, clarifying that their actions had driven Eddie into a rage. With a small sigh, she described how she had been raped and beaten afterwards, effectively forced to take her place among the group.

After that, the entire group went back on the road, and Tori described her duties, both the ones that everyone saw and knew about, and the secret ones she became as apt at performing. "I became a murdering whore," she shrugged, "I have learned to accept that about myself. And worked to change it."

Brian cringed at her words, and she stared at him coldly, "I warned you it was bad. I told you that you could not forget it after it was shared."

"I know, I know," he agreed with a nod. "It's not *how bad* it was that has me. It's how coldly you talk about it. If it weren't for the tiny tear here and there, it would be like you couldn't give a shit less one way or the other."

She stared at him. *Holy fuck, he hasn't figured it out. And I even told him before... I told him I borrow people's feelings.* "Yeah well, I guess I'm just good at hiding things. Anyways, that's about it. So, I guess we're done here?" She smiled as if she had been telling them about visiting summer camp.

"Uh, no," Collin interceded. "You've told us lots of crap about things that happened and you did, and I will be the first to admit it's pretty fucked up. But you still haven't told us why those things make it so dangerous for you to go public."

"Yeah," Brian sided with him, "Now tell me why you can't join the band. Those guys are dead. Your past is behind you."

Shaking her head slowly from side to side, she spoke in a low tone, "There are others. Many others. Who knows what they saw or think they know about me. If I surface publicly, it will only be a matter of time before they come after me, and then all of you will be in danger. I can't take that risk. I never wanted you to be found in the first place. I wanted to keep you safe."

Staring at her, Brian could not believe his ears. "You mean you weren't looking for me?" he asked dubiously.

"No, I wasn't looking for you. And honestly, I think that's why the Feds went to all that trouble to alter my age. They claimed they were searching for my family, but in the wrong age bracket, so my identity would never have been found. As it turns out, I was never registered as a missing child, so it was a moot point. I didn't want you to be found so

The Organization could never use you against me, or hurt you to get to me."

"The way the Scorpions did," Brian finished for her.

"Exactly. We were so lucky then, you have no idea how it could have turned out." Her face grim, the three friends had a much better understanding than she realized.

"But no, to answer your question, I had no intention of ever looking for my lost family. It was purely an accident that Brett knew enough about how I was acquired to locate you and tear up your house." Glancing around the room, she recalled their previous visit to the location and the discovery of her identity.

"He only wanted to draw me out; after getting to know him, I don't think he would have really hurt you. He wasn't quite like the leader of the Dragons and his group was more or less soft."

The guys had a cynical laugh at the fact she called a group of cold-blooded killers *soft*.

Exhausted in the telling of her story, and having said all she intended to say, Tori stood and left the group of men to ponder her words and talk amongst themselves. Making her way up to her room, she ignored the bag of items she had been packing that remained on her bed. Instead, she turned left past the bathroom that lay on the left as you entered the suite.

Making her way down beside the bed, she sank to her knees and placed her right shoulder into the corner. Resting her forehead against the wall, she breathed deeply for several minutes, listening to the silence. She had never intended to have another soul know about the life she had lived; about her darkest hours. Before she finally fell asleep, she had time to curse the sheriff and his deputies who had rescued her in Iowa and wished to God they could have been a few minutes later.

To Have and To Hold

Tori awoke the next morning to find her husband lying on the bed, staring at her. Shifting, she turned so that her back pressed into the corner and she could look at him more squarely. Saying nothing, she simply waited to hear whatever he had to say.

Michael had been watching her since he had come up the stairs, not having been to sleep yet. The group of men had talked for several hours after she had left them, and he had felt obliged to stay and hear what they had to say about her tale. Eventually, he had shared his own dark part in the way they had met, and why he had come to live with the band as their personal protection.

"I watched them abuse her. Like she said, she was their whore, and that's all I knew," Michael filled in some of the blanks for the group of men. "My brother tried to clue me in, but he wouldn't give me details. Made me promise to look after her when he sent her to me, only Eddie killed him before he could make that happen. It was only by dumb luck or a twist of fate that our paths crossed and I got a second chance to make good on my word."

"Anyways, it was Eddie who sent me to be head of security here. Apparently, he had been keeping tabs on Brian for years and saw the opening as an opportunity to get a better hold on him."

Collin laughed, "Yeah, that was a ballsy move, sending you to watch the girl's brother."

"Yes it was, but he never lacked for balls. Eddie was a damn smart man. Never did anything without purpose. He probably made only one mistake in his whole twisted plot; he picked a little girl smarter and more stubborn than him, and she clearly beat him in the end."

Lying on their bed, looking at her, he wondered if she knew she had already won. "I guess you know you beat them. The only power any of those guys have over you is the power you give them."

Tori stared at him, blinking slowly and turning his words in her mind.

"By letting your fear get the better of you," he continued, "You're losing part of that victory. Don't get me wrong, I love you more than anything, and what I want most is to take you home, to make babies with you, and raise them in that huge house we bought and are restoring." He noticed her small smile at the image he described, so he finished the thought, "But deep down, I know that life would be a lie."

Her smile disappeared, her brow wrinkled in pain, "It's not a lie; I love you, too, and I want those things as badly as you do."

Michael raised his chin as a challenge, "Maybe. I mean, I really want to believe that, but deep down, I keep thinking that this life is the truth. This life is your destiny." He pointed an extended digit at her, "After you left, your brother said some things. Got me to thinking in a way I really hadn't. Things I hadn't really wanted to face." He didn't want to tell her the men had argued over her again before he finally began to see the reality behind his actions and those of the other man.

"He has an interesting way of seeing things. If Eddie

Farrell hadn't interfered, you would probably have found your place in your brother's band a long time ago. You have a talent that is so clear. Yeah, you're good at lots of things, but playing is the one that moves you. It shows in your eyes and on your face, when you hold a guitar and make it sing, telling all the things your spirit wants to say."

"Wow, Marge was right," Tori leaned her head back against the wall, "You are a smooth talker."

"Yeah," Michael laughed, "I guess I can be. But no more than you." His eyes twinkled slightly as he relished in their connection. "The guys, they know it's the truth. After you left, Collin and Brian said you used to play in Terry's shop, alone, like you were hiding and keeping it all for yourself. And it's evident every time you put your hands on the strings; that is the time that you are truly alive."

"So what're you saying? That means I *have* to join the band?"

He stared at her for a long moment, his turn to consider his words carefully before he spit them out. "Ok, yeah, that's what I'm saying. You have to join the band," he stated flatly. "It's what you were meant to do. And no one is afraid of having people come after them because of your past. No one, except you." He stared at her, waiting for her to protest, but she held her tongue and glared back at him.

"So you guys aren't even the least bit afraid of what could happen?" she finally asked in a quiet voice.

Sitting up, he tried to be honest, "I think we're all more afraid of choosing out of fear. I would love to take you home, but I need you to be there because that's the life you want, not because you were too afraid to take the one you were born to have."

She stared at him, taking shallow breaths as she considered his plea. Deciding to take another track, she shook her head, "How is that fair to you? You and I are supposed to be building a life together, a life we started in a little town in Texas. How is it fair if I just change those plans on a whim, because my brother asked me too?"

Michael didn't even flinch, "Who said life was fair? You of all people should know that it isn't."

Seeing her resolve weakening, he pushed on. "I took you to have and to hold, for richer or for poorer, in sickness and in health, until death do we part. I meant those words. I meant the ones that are engraved inside your ring. I loved our life in Texas, but I love you more. Wherever you go, I will be by your side. And you don't have to worry about the bad guys coming after you. I'm gonna be there if they ever do. I got your back, baby girl, and don't you ever forget it."

Standing, he left her, still leaning in the corner and thinking about what he had said. Making his way into the bathroom, he closed the door behind him. Stripping down, he turned on the shower and climbed beneath the hot spray.

Placing his head against the smooth tile, he felt weary from his long night and the heavy thoughts that plagued his heart and mind. Not hearing the door open and close, he jumped slightly when the curtain moved, and his wife stepped into the tub behind him.

Smiling at him, she admonished, "You know you're not allowed to call me *baby girl*. That was Henry's name for me."

Giving her a small grimace, he countered, "Well, you think he was raising you for Eddie, but he wasn't. My brother was making you for me."

She grinned, considering that thought for a moment, knowing he could probably be right. Reaching up, she ran her hand over his slumped shoulder.

Michael turned to face her. Taking her in his arms, they shared a deep kiss and he shifted to plant her firmly, back against the wall. Relaxing her leg, she allowed him access to her soft hollow, and he took her beneath the warm cascade as he had always done when they were together and naked. *She really is the perfect woman for me.*

Not So Fast

After their steamy encounter, the couple drew the drapes to hold out the day, stretched out on the bed and slept for several hours. Awakening before her husband, Tori spooned up behind him, her arm draped around his chest to feel him breathe.

The room dimly lit, the sun had traveled well into afternoon, still held out by the dark shades that were pulled across the glass. Breathing into his hair, her love for him consumed her, and she hoped that he would not pay for his words with his life; or anyone else's.

Stroking his curling hairs heavily, she roused him gently, and they made love again before they dressed and made their way down the stairs. The other band members had also slept in, accustomed to the late to bed and late to rise way of life. Still not completely convinced this was where she belonged, Tori had at least become willing to talk about it.

Taking a cup from the cabinet, she reached for the pot of coffee, and Michael watched her with a raised brow. He had only seen her drink anything other than water a few times in his life. Sipping the hot liquid, he could tell she wanted to calm herself before they began the conversation that she dreaded. Still facing the cabinet, standing next to the sink, she began.

"So, what exactly is it you guys have in mind?" she asked the question about nothing specific, wanting to give them a chance to talk about whatever meant the most to them.

Sensing they may have reached a point of gaining her consent, Brian spoke up, "We want you, of course. We think you would be a great addition to the group."

Shaking her head, she countered, "Not good enough. There's lots of musicians who could do that." Turning around and leaning her rear end against the counter, coffee mug in hand, she raised it towards Collin and put the question to him. "What do you think about all of this?" She glared at him, waiting for him to respond.

Staring at his friend's sister, he thought about the time he had taken her to his hotel room, with the intent of getting her sloppy drunk and doing every nasty thing he could think of to her. After finally hearing her story, he felt relieved he had not succeeded. In a submissive voice he replied, "I think we would be damned lucky to have you," and left it at that.

Cutting her eyes over at Cody, she did not bother to repeat the query.

Clearing his throat, "I only hope you remember that *I am* the lead singer," he thumped his chest at the words *I am*, "Because you have a great voice and I would really like to keep my job." Something in his smile made her heart skip a beat and she considered that he might have been serious.

Nodding slowly, she countered, "Not so fast. I haven't agreed to anything yet."

Brian showed his full set of perfect white teeth, hearing the word *yet*, and extrapolating she hadn't, but she was going to.

"I wanna know what's in it for me," she finished, her tone gruff as she tried to play off her growing desire to agree to the move.

Collin's turn to show off his conceit, he joked in a booming voice, "You get to be a part of the best band ever. What more could you want?"

The other two men laughed at his bold move, and Tori herself had to smile. She had found him so annoying, the way he pursued her back in LA. His response typical for him, she praised herself for not giving in to his advances, especially since they were going to be working together.

"Well, then I guess I have to go for it, right?" she spoke slowly, trying not to appear too eager. "So, what's the plan?" wondering exactly what she had signed herself up for.

The group spent the rest of the afternoon going over their itinerary for the next six months, as the tour had already been scheduled to begin before summer came. Pointing out that they may have started having cancelations in light of the accident, they decided the time had come to give Mark Holt a call and let him in on the good news.

Their manager seemed a bit surprised at their decision to shift everyone around to make a spot for Tori in the position of guitarist. Since he had not been present to hear her play at her one and only public performance, he could be heard noisily chattering while Cody patiently listened.

Hanging up his cell, Cody informed them, "Suffice it to say, he's not pleased with the choice being made without his input, and he suggested he be allowed to hear her play before any final verdicts are made."

Tori laughed at the way the singer mocked the man and his attitude, scoffing his lack of faith in her band mates' judgment.

"Regardless," Cody went on, "He lives in Manhattan, and will be over shortly to hear what you can do."

Looking at each of the men in turn, Tori considered the possibilities, the wheels inside turning. Silently, she planned how she would make the man feel like the jerk he was being, and headed off to the small studio to get to work.

Tori looked over the selection of guitars that her brother had. Her black and white one still at the house in Texas, she thought about insisting they would have to retrieve it before she made any real music. However, for today, she would use a couple of his to complete her prank on the man who doubted her ability and would be arriving shortly to hear for himself.

Taking two of them, she tuned one perfectly and set it on the stand ready to go. Lifting the second one, she made sure none of the strings held the right tone, and she would sound perfectly horrid when she strummed them.

Watching her curiously, Brian finally asked, "Why are you doing that?"

Giving him an evil grin, she barked an odd laugh, "Well, I can't stab him, but I'm sure I can inflict at least a little bit of pain before I show him what I can really do."

He only shook his head, not really understanding his sister's sick sense of humor.

A short time later, Mark arrived at the house. Meeting him at the front door, Brian tried not to spoil her surprise as he led their manager to the studio, where everyone else had gathered, playing around on their instruments and brainstorming ideas. Seeing him enter the room, Tori traded her guitar for her special surprise.

Adjusting the strap, she took on a nervous stance and darted her eyes around from person to person, waiting for the cue to begin her assault.

Mark didn't even smile at her, not believing her to be anything more than an interloper. "Ok," he commanded with a loud, exasperated sigh, "Let's hear the cover title."

Giving her brother a slow grin, Tori ran through the cords, which, in fact, did sound pretty horrid. Adding insult to injury, she further butchered the riffs by failing to mute strings and periodically held her fingers out of position so that they were not compressed properly.

Hearing her fiasco, her new band mates began to snicker. Collin covered his mouth trying to stifle his, and then snorted out his nose, which sent all three of them into hysterics.

Indignation covering his face, Mark demanded sharply, "What's so fucking funny? She's terrible!" he stammered in a shocked tone, "How could you guys even consider this?"

Tori's turn to smile, she sat down the instrument, and traded it for the better quality one that had been waiting patiently on the little wire rack. Coolly, she adjusted the new instrument into position, and in a condescending tone replied for them, "Maybe because they don't need you telling them what's good."

Not waiting for him to respond, she opened up with the introduction, her fingers prancing across the strings perfectly. His mouth slightly open, he listened as she produced incredible sounds, her hair falling forward as she shifted during her performance, riff after riff coming to life.

Nodding as she played, the guys appeared entirely pleased at her ability and were grateful she had come around to do her part in the end. Finishing the piece, Tori reached up, catching her hair by running her fingers up her forehead and pushing it back while tossing it behind her.

Brian remembered seeing the move back in LA, when they first surprised her, and had discovered her hidden talent. *She even has a signature move,* the thought made him grin.

Giving her an angry glare, Mark stated in a brackish tone, "I guess you think you're cute, don't you." Glancing at Collin, he considered that she might actually be more arrogant than the drummer, and understood that this could make for some interesting times in the future. "Ok," he then relented, "I guess she'll do."

Eager to finalize the plans for the album and the tour, the group spent the rest of the evening discussing their current agenda and any changes that would need to be made. Right away, Tori pointed out that she wasn't doing any of it if she had to leave Michael behind, giving her mate a hungry stare as she spoke. They decided there would actually be room for him on their bus if the couple didn't mind riding with the rest of the guys.

Not wanting to make things too difficult, she agreed that would be acceptable. Keeping her fears under cover, she actually felt quite nervous about the whole affair, and not because she thought they would be in danger.

Tori had never been one to stand out in a crowd. She had learned early on that quiet and meek went far on the road, and she wasn't sure how well she would do up against the three men and their purely dominant personalities.

Running her fingers through her hair, she also voiced her concern about alcohol consumption. At hearing this, the group fell silent, waiting for her to elaborate on exactly what she thought.

Inhaling deeply, Tori quickly decided to get to the point, and stated flatly, "I'm an alcoholic. I really have no desire to return to it, either. I got lucky when I went after the Scorpions, consuming a great deal during that time, but being able to put it away when I returned home, largely because there was no further temptation in my life."

Giving them a moment to process what she was getting at, she continued, "I know you guys are going to want to party on as you always have, but I really don't want to dive head first into that lifestyle." Stopping there, she hoped that her intent had been made clear as the group buzzed for several minutes, tossing around ideas while Michael beamed with pride at his wife's forethought.

"I think we need a different bus," Brian finally offered. "Maybe one that has a sub-compartment in the back, like a regular bedroom. That way they can be alone and away from the rest of us when we are doing our thing."

Nodding their agreement, Cody and Collin thought that would be a valid suggestion for allowing Tori to have more privacy and maintain a certain distance from the things that concerned her.

Having that settled, the group also addressed the issue of publicity. Their newest member might also raise some eyebrows out in their fan base, and they needed a way to show that she wasn't just some girl, or that she actually could play and had earned her spot. They then decided they wanted to appear on a late night television show as a way of announcing she would be joining the group.

"Hey, you know," Cody piped up, "She could also do like a cover shoot or something. Like, have photographs made of her and of us together, for like promotional stuff."

Tori made a face, and glancing around the group, she informed them that she wasn't very accustomed to being photographed and wasn't sure she wanted to start now.

Mark had been making notes of the suggestions and putting his two cents in where appropriate. At her comment, he looked up from his scribbles to stare at her. Working with the girl would definitely be a challenge, especially if she always needed persuading to do things.

Stretching in a dramatic fashion, she chose that point to announce she felt ready to call it a night. Michael followed her up the stairs, leaving the remaining four men to discuss what had transpired and make further plans. Catching up to her as she entered their bedroom, he closed the door behind them and gave her a broad smile.

"I think you're making a good choice," he spoke softly

as he reached for her, "I have a really good feeling about this."

Tori ran her hands up his spine, suddenly not the least bit interested in anything other than getting naked and partaking in her favorite pastime with her lover.

Out in the Open

Eli clutched a folder as he strutted down the hall. *Man, if it weren't for bad breaks, this case wouldn't be getting any breaks at all*. Arriving at the conference room, he pushed the door open and made his way inside.

"Ah, there he is," Special Agent James Godfry spoke in his clear, resonating tone. "You have the file?"

"Yes, sir; right here," he approached the set of tables, handing the folder across to his superior while taking note that La Buff and some new guy were both present at the briefing. Agent Founder felt his entire body grow tense, seeing the map Tori had used to guide the group along her journey of murder and mayhem spread across the tables. *And the hits just keep on coming.*

Noticing his keen eye, Jim lay the newest file next to the few others lying on the table with the map. "We are refreshing ourselves on the details that she gave us, assessing our progress on the situation. Notice the new red markings across the black? Those are confirmed locations. We have put together files on each."

Eli nodded, "Yes, so we essentially are only a few spots away from having this locked down. With what I have there in my contribution, we should be all set."

"Good," the newcomer boomed with a deep voice,

"It's about time we made some real headway here." He moved up next to the table, giving Eli a disapproving glare.

"Special Agent Founder, this is Special Agent Mason Hunt. He's joining our group, since we seem to be growing a little short on members," Jim did not smile as he spoke.

"Yes, sir; I heard. What happened, exactly?" Eli's frustration peeking through his façade, "I thought things were going smoothly."

"They were going smoothly," the newest member chimed in, "Until all hell broke loose!" Jim gave him a sideways look, which he ignored. "Acquiring this girl is likely to get us all killed if we aren't careful. Now, I am prepared to go get her. This latest incident just goes to show, we aren't handling this situation correctly - "

"That's enough!" Godfry cut him off. "You may be on the team, but I'm still in charge here, and *we* aren't going to do anything. This latest incident only goes to show that forces are in motion. Forces that cannot always be seen or predicted."

Eli looked at his feet, *I wish to God I knew what was going on.* Reaching over, he flipped open the file folder bearing Doug Seeming's name, exposing a small stack of photographs; the top image knocked the wind out of him and he emitted a sharp cry as if in pain, *holy shit!*

Slowly, Jim's hand closed the folder, "Yes, it's pretty gruesome. The funeral will be tomorrow. And of course, it's pretty safe to assume that whatever he knew is out in the open."

Eli's head popped up, eyes wide with concern, "Oh my God, what about Tori? He knew where she was. Is. He knew everything. We have to do something! We have to -"

"Calm down, son," Jim raised a hand to cut him off, "We're working on details, putting a plan together. However, I can assure you, we aren't going to interfere here any longer." He gave Mason a sideways glance.

"You two will go, shadow her. You will NOT make contact, nor will you interfere should anyone make a move against her. From now on, we are response only, as far as the girl is concerned. Let this run its course, follow the snakes home when they slither away."

"You mean use her as bait!?!" Eli's eyes flashed in anger.

"She made her choice. We offered to let her in, make her part of the team… she chose to walk away. So be it. Like I said, you two can shadow her but don't interfere. And keep me posted." Jim's face looked grave. She did save Tommy after all, so he wasn't any happier about it than Eli was.

Sneak Peek at Intrepid

Book 6 of A New Life Series

Enrique ran his fingers around the outside of his mouth, considering the other man's words. "Alright, let's head south. But we gotta be sure we can leave quick, in case she needs us."

"Agreed," Brett grabbed his gear off the table and stood. "Riding in snow is jus' plain stupid, ya know. Ya got your gloves?"

"Yeah, I got 'em. Hate wearing 'em. They don't feels right."

Brett grinned, "Like frostbite's gonna feel any better."

Enrique followed the older man to the front of the shop, pulling out his protective wear. He stopped to lean on the counter, "At least the wind's died down. We gos straight south from here I guess."

"Yup," Brett swung around, his gaze sliding over the wide expanse of colorful magazine covers next to him. Immediately he did a double take, *what the fuck?* Retracing the path his eyes had traveled, he muttered to himself, *guess I must miss 'er more than I thought… seeing 'er on the front of the tabloids.*

His heart began to pound when he caught the image again. "Hey! We got trouble!" he slapped the other man on the arm to get his attention.

"Man, we always gots trouble. What're you talkin' about?" Enrique chuckled while shaking his head, following the leader's finger as it pointed. Taking in the photograph of the four figures, he gasped aloud, "No fucking way. No way in hells she'd be that stupid." His hand reaching to grasp the issue, Brett fumbled in his pocket to give the clerk another twenty.

Moving off to the side, he flipped the slick pages with his anxious fingers, finding an article about the group. "Oh my God, this's real," Enrique read aloud, *"Tori Anderson, sister of Brian Madson, is joining the band, but can she fill the void?"*

"Well, there goes our plans for some place warm," Brett shook his red curls violently, "Come on, we gotta roll." Swinging around, he made for the door, "We'll start with that place o' theirs in Jersey."

"Wait! You mean we're going now? Before she even calls us?" Enrique's voice squeaked slightly.

"Yeah, we go now. If anything actually happens, she won' get a chance t' call."

The Band Played On

Tori clenched her fingers, feeling her tenseness ease slightly as they pressed against her mate's. *Deep breath, baby girl. You're gonna be fine.* Smiling at the man next to her, he returned her grin, and she leaned over to give him a small kiss.

"You nervous?" he prodded gently in German, unable to tell by her placid expression.

"Little bit," she replied in kind, "But I think it's going to be ok."

"Sure it is," he gave her hand a shake, "You've got nothing to worry about." He could feel Peter Farside's disgruntled glare upon him as he spoke.

The couple sat in the back of the limo, with the rest of the band in the center, surrounding the bar and enjoying the ride with their typical, boyish banter. Having reached the first week of December, the group has a small gig that will air on a late night program to announce the change in the line-up. The band's newest head of security languished on the far end of the car, only there because Michael had insisted that he come.

Brian took note of her flat calm, nodding his approval,

"No sweat, sis. This's a piece of cake," he called out, flashing his teeth for effect.

Everything had been kept hush-hush up to that point, but they knew if they delayed for long, the story would get out somehow. Taking Cody's suggestion to heart, the group had hired a photojournalist, who had taken a spread of pictures for them the previous morning in preparation for the media blitz that would follow the broadcast.

This appearance is the first step; the first hurdle. We make it today, and it's all downhill from here; Tori reassured herself. The photographer had been a real pro, putting the girl at ease and getting a wide range of shots that would be used by various magazines. They in turn would be providing coverage and publicity for the group.

Using an authoritative voice, her brother explained the day's agenda in detail, "The audience isn't very big. And, according to plan, we don't have to do anything but play. That's easy. We go out, do our thing, and we're done." He gave her a small chuckle, happy that things had worked out, and she could be so close.

"I know, Danny. I'm fine. Like yesterday, I got this covered." She smiled at his concern, hoping it really turned out that simple.

Arriving at the studio, the group made their way inside. Tori drew a deep breath, vaguely surprised by the number of people snapping more pictures of them as they exited the car and entered the building. "Wow, I guess I wasn't expecting that kind of welcome."

"It's a fact of life," Collin pointed out in a clipped tone, "Famous people get in pictures. Don't sweat it," he commanded, "You look great." He let the compliment land easily, and it gave Tori a few butterflies that he thought so, considering their past.

208

The studio being a familiar stop for the band, they were accustomed to the hustle and bustle of the industry, and that afforded her a small amount of comfort. She may not have been acquainted with what would be going on, but the rest of the guys were. If anything wasn't what it should be, they would let her know.

Dropping his bride off at the green room with the others, Michael gave her a small kiss, "Break a leg, baby girl." Leaning his forehead against hers, he rocked her side to side for a moment, "I'll see you after the show."

"Yeah," she exhaled a small puff of air, "No worries, love; I'm fine."

Leaving her, he made his way down the hall, following Pete as he lumbered along. All old hat for Michael, he knew he wanted to have a look at the crowd. Frowning, he stopped next to the man who stood five inches shorter and at least fifty pounds heavier, noticing he had begun preparing a cup of coffee. "You're not gonna have a look around?" his voice dripped with disdain.

Waving his stir stick, the other man replied curtly, "Why? The studio's got security. What's there to be afraid of?" His brow held deep lines, his displeasure at being told how to do his job obvious.

Michael scowled but said nothing, leaving him to his refreshments. Reaching the stage area, he mentally walked through the conversation he had had with Pete the day before. *He has a hands off approach;* he recalled, *putting technology and other people in charge of the group's well-being. With any other band, he might get away with that.*

His eyes made a pass across the smiling faces, and he moved against the wall. Michael didn't like the man's attitude one bit; *he's fat and lazy, in my book. Some things you have to see and do for yourself.* He wasn't ready to ask for his old job back, but he was getting close, the reasons fresh on his mind.

Michael knew that deep down, Tori feared being recognized, and he understood why. *The possibility that it could happen exists, however slim it might be, and that's only part of the danger.* He knew the others didn't fully appreciate those things, but that was ok, he had her back.

Intrepid is Available Now!

About the Author

Anyone who knows me could tell you, I am a friendly kind of person, never met a stranger and take up conversations anywhere at any time. I work hard, and my mind never seems to shut down, as I wake up often in the middle of the night with ideas pouring out and demanding to be dealt with. Of course that means much of my books were written in the middle of the night.

I grew up and still live in the great state of Texas where everything is bigger, where we have warm weather and a central location. I love my state, my town, and my family, which includes my four sons, my significant other, and many friends as well.

I have thoroughly enjoyed writing this story and hope that you will love reading it just as much. And of course, there will be many more adventures to come.

You can follow Samantha Jacobey at:
Website: www.SamJacobey.com
Facebook: https://www.facebook.com/SamJacobey
Twitter: https://twitter.com/SamJacobey
Pinterest: http://www.pinterest.com/samanthajacobey/

Other works by Samantha Jacobey

http://www.amazon.com/-/e/B00GEB5LX0

Summer Spirit Novella Series - no one EVER had a summer romance like this… Charlie visits another plane, parallel to our own, where Summer Angels and Dark Angels battle over the fate of man. A unique twist on an old idea that will keep you guessing; will Charlie and Clarisse ever find their HEA? (New adult)

Irrevocable Series – from affluent beginnings, BAILEY DEWITT's life has become a broken mess... after her parents died unexpectedly, she didn't think it could get any worse. But when the arrogance of man catches up and puts the entire world into a dooms-day spiral, there will be only ONE PLACE she can run to... the ONE PLACE she wanted desperately to escape.... (New Adult)

Teach Me to Prey – in this standalone thriller, JASON TRUITT and his friends have gotten their way for years. Deceit, sex, and foul play aren't normally covered in the curriculum, but they're doing whatever it takes to get under BECKY STEWART's skin. When one of the boys turns up dead, it's a race against time to save the others; a STUNNING STORY that will get your heart racing and leave you breathless by the end… (New Adult)

The Wicked Awakened – a Halloween novel, a five hundred year old witch wants to turn SARAH MATTHEWS' body into her new home… A twisted tale involving a coven hell bent on seeing that she succeeds. Who will come out on top in this epic battle of wills? (Mature read, 18+ for sexual content and violence)

www.ingramcontent.com/pod-product-compliance
Lightning Source LLC
Chambersburg PA
CBHW030315180626
46810CB00003B/1088